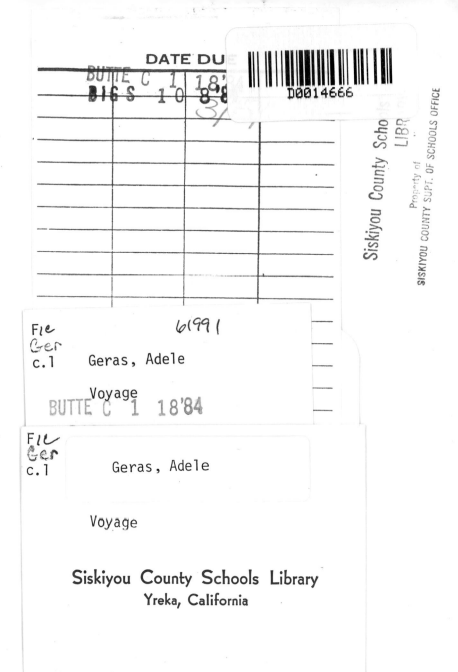

Books by Adèle Geras

The Girls in the Velvet Room
Other Echoes
Apricots at Midnight
Voyage

VOYAGE

VOYAGE

Adèle Geras

Atheneum   *1983*   *New York*

LIBRARY OF CONGRESS CATALOGING IN PUBLICATION DATA
Geras, Adèle.   Voyage.
SUMMARY: *Relates the experiences of a group of
young people in the early twentieth century as
they journey from their homes in Eastern Europe
to the United States in search of
a new life.*
[*1. Voyages and travel—Fiction. 2. United States—
Emigration and immigration—Fiction*] *I. Title.*
PZ7.G29354Vo 1983   [Fic]   82-13760
ISBN 0-689-30955-4

Published simultaneously in Canada by
McClelland & Stewart, Ltd.
Composition by Service Typesetters, Austin, Texas
Printed and bound by Fairfield Graphics,
Fairfield, Pennsylvania
Designed and decorated by Marge Zaum
First Edition

For Elise

Note

In the thirty years before the outbreak of the First World War, thousands upon thousands of people, many of them Jews, left their homelands, fleeing from the oppression, persecution and poverty that was their lot in much of Eastern Europe. A large number of them went to America, looking for a new kind of life. The story that follows is set in November, 1904. The characters bear no relation to any real person, and, as far as I know, there was no real ship called the *S. S. Danzig*.

VOYAGE

Chapter 1

THEY HAD BROUGHT ALL THEIR TREASURES WITH THEM: silver candlesticks, tablecloths embroidered in the yellow lamplight on long winter evenings, books bound in leather, jewelry if they had any, feather pillows, blankets, everything they could cram into their bundles and suitcases. Scuffed and battered and dirty, these were, and if they survived the voyage, some of them, it would be a miracle.

Mina had brought paper, as much of it as she could fit into the baggage. It slipped in comfortably between sheets and clothes and along the sides of the case. Old school books of Eli's, only partly used, scraps torn from the bottom of letters, calendars from long ago, anything. Anything that she could draw on. She was drawing now, leaning on the suitcase. The paper had creases across it from being folded and stuck inside her boot. It wasn't very clean, either; but dirt was something Mina had quickly become used to on this journey, because it was everywhere and there was nothing you could do about it, although some tried.

Mina sketched in Golda's face as she leaned over and spoke to Rachel. Thick hair the color of chestnuts curled from beneath a hat of shiny blue velveteen, and her gloves were still quite clean. She had pink cheeks, and shiny, pointed leather boots, only a little cracked. She sat on a cardboard suitcase, cradling a tiny baby in her arms and leaning on a huge bundle of sheets and blankets as though it were a plump sofa strewn with satin cushions. Mina was almost tempted to draw in a table and an oil lamp at her side.

Rachel sat very still, her arms around her knees. A scarf hid her fair hair. She was looking down. Mina imagined her standing in a wide field, green behind her as far as the eye could see, no trees, no wind, silence. What was she thinking? Maybe if Golda ever stopped talking (about her husband, mainly, waiting for her in America, and about how she would decorate this room and that room, and how, when she had the money one day, she would dress herself and the baby . . .) Rachel would say something. Mina knew, from Rachel's clear eyes, from the smile that seemed somehow just ready to be smiled, waiting in the up-turned corners of her wide mouth, that what she said would be worth waiting for.

Golda and Rachel were grown-up. Only three or

four years older than me, thought Mina, and already women. Will I know so much when I am seventeen or eighteen, about dress lengths and fashions and furniture? Do I really want to? Mina drew in the baby's tiny nose. How can a nose be so small, she wondered. And fingers moving like pink sea creatures. This pencil isn't fine enough. She stopped drawing and listened. Golda said:

". . . you must put all that behind you now. How can you live in the past? You're only seventeen. It's a hard thing to say, Rachel, but I have to say it. It was a tragedy, and God preserve us all from such things, but to hide behind it like a wall, never to look, or think of finding someone else, a fine girl like you . . . It's a sin."

(What was a tragedy? Mina asked herself. No wonder Rachel was silent.)

"I have to look after my father," said Rachel calmly. "Without my mother, who has he got?"

Golda snorted. "He is, forgive me, a grown man. Perhaps he can look after himself a little, too. And grandchildren? Won't he want grandchildren?"

"I'm only seventeen," Rachel said. "Nearly eighteen."

"Is seventeen so young? Look at me. Only nineteen, and I feel like an old woman sometimes, believe me. My baby is a month old already. Look at that girl over there. She can't be any older than you, and her baby will probably be born on the ship, poor thing. That I don't envy her, I can tell you, but still, there she is." Rachel opened her mouth, but Golda did not pause for a moment.

Mina stopped listening, and looked at the dazed, vacant eyes and huge, round stomach of the pregnant woman. She seemed to be traveling alone. Or maybe not. There was someone now, taking her arm, taking her to sit somewhere. An old man. The girl followed him as if in a dream, not smiling. Soon she was swallowed up in the crowd, and Mina lost sight of her. She looked at the open door of the huge shed. Just above the dark triangular shapes of the roofs outside, you could see a small pale gray rectangle of sky, the first light of a November morning. Voices made a river of sound: questions and cries and sighs and the thin whimpering of children who had not eaten but were too exhausted to shout swirled like water all around her.

Her mother's shrieks (had her heart been torn from her body, or what?) sliced through other noises like great, silver scissors, and Mina felt her body stiffen, as Hannah pushed through the crowd and sank to her knees.

"Mama, what is it? What's the matter? Please, Mama, stop shrieking like that. Stop. It doesn't help. Calm down. Tell me. Please tell me."

Hannah Isaacs put both hands over her trembling mouth. Strands of graying hair fell over her forehead. Her shawl had been dragged along the floor.

"I can't find Eli."

"Oh, Mama, how could you lose him now? Where did you see him last? We're nearly ready to go, why didn't you . . ." The words faded from Mina's lips as she fought down her impatience. I mustn't blame her, she thought, she's upset. She's tired. But it's not fair. I have to do everything. I have to look after Eli the whole time, or this is what happens. I'm like the mother and she's like the daughter, and it's not fair. I'm only fourteen. Why should I have to worry all the time? And Eli—where is he? Mina folded the paper and tucked it into her boot with the pencil.

"I'll find him, Mama, don't worry. Stay here. I'll find him. Don't move from here. I'll come back."

"But if they call us? To check documents, or tickets, or money?"

Mina shouted, "I don't care if an archangel calls you to the Seat of Judgement, just don't move from here! How do you expect me to find you again if you move around? Have you seen what's going on here? Look at the people: shoved together like cows. Hundreds. Maybe more. Just don't move. And don't cry. I'll find him. Really, Mama, I'll find him. I'm going now."

Rachel put an arm round Hannah's shoulders. "Don't worry, Mina," she said. "We'll take care of her."

Mina nodded, turned, and began to elbow her way through the mass of bodies.

"Eli!" she shouted. "Eli, where are you? It's Mina. Eli, where are you?" She looked into the faces of children: this one had a blue jacket, that one had thin legs just like her brother's, but they were strangers, and they looked at Mina with blank eyes, unresisting even when she pulled at their shoulders. They were used to being shouted at and pushed, driven from this train to that hall, and finally to the shed on the dockside. Nothing could startle them.

But where is he, he must be here somewhere, thought Mina, and then: what if I can't find him? What if he's wandered out of the shed, fallen into the water, drowned . . .

"Eli," she shouted. "Eli, where are you?" She stumbled over bundles and baskets, suitcases and bags, bumping into brown backs and gray legs, and tripping over small children. For an eternity, it seemed, she pushed and ran and shouted Eli's name. Her own voice sounded cracked and hoarse in her ears, and she heard her mother's wailing as clearly as though there were complete silence all around.

"Hey! Hey, you! Carrot-top, hey! Ginger!" She's shouting at me, thought Mina, and for a moment rage made her forget her brother, and she turned towards the voice, ready to scream at whoever it was, hit them if necessary.

"Is this brat the one you're looking for?"

"Eli! Oh, thank God. Where have you been? Why did you leave Mama? Didn't I tell you and tell you?" She pulled Eli roughly to her side, and put an arm round him, tight, tight, to keep him safe.

The woman who had found her and brought Eli back had a mean, complaining mouth with too few teeth. Her son stood beside her, an ugly, heavy child with pale eyes.

"I'm very grateful to you for finding him and looking after him," Mina said, and added inwardly: and

I'll even forgive the remarks about my hair. The woman sniffed. "As if I hadn't enough to worry about. As if they don't make make things difficult enough. And who could get a word out of him? He'll be nothing but a burden to you, let me tell you. Didn't you know there's a rule? They don't let idiots, mental defectives, into America."

"He's not an idiot. He gets easily confused. He's shy. Upset."

"He's crying," said the boy, sneering. "He's mad. He'll be sent back on the next boat, you'll see."

Mina swung out a foot and kicked the boy's shin as hard as she could.

"For shame, you horrible child. How dare you talk like that?"

"Don't you touch my son, you bad-tempered girl. I should have known, with your hair. That's all I need. My poor baby . . . did she hurt you?"

"Leave my hair out of it, you wicked woman," Mina shouted. "I know your kind of person. Nothing but a busybody and a moaner, and your precious child is a bully. There should be laws stopping moaners and bullies into America, so there. Come on, Eli, we're going. Who needs to mix with such people?" She pulled her brother by the hand so hard that he almost fell.

"Mina . . ." Her mother's voice floated to her over the crowd. Looking up, she could just see Hannah's head above the rest. She must be standing on a suitcase, thought Mina. Please God don't let it burst. Not now.

"I've found him," she yelled as loudly as she could.

"Wait there. I'm coming."

She knelt down beside her brother and spoke gently to him. "Why did you wander away? You mustn't. Didn't I tell you? Why did you?"

Eli frowned. "I don't remember. I was walking around. I was looking at things."

"Well, no more walking and looking. Do you understand? Stay with me. Or Mama. Always. Do you understand?"

"Yes," said Eli. Mina looked into his eyes. Brown eyes, lovely eyes, deep. What did he see with them, Mina wondered. What did things look like to him? He wasn't mad. That dreadful woman, how did she dare? Not mad, but she knew that what Eli saw and understood was his own world, not like the world that other people saw. He understood different things, that was all. Sometimes it took a lot of talking, but in the end he understood. In his way.

Eli was a little different from other children, that was all. Sometimes you spoke to him and he looked straight through you as if you weren't there, as if for those few moments, he was unconscious of everything. Then, later, when he was talking again and listening again, it became clear that he had heard nothing you'd been saying during that short time of blankness.

Once, angrily, she had said: "Eli, you haven't been attending at all. What have I just been saying? Go on. Tell me."

And Eli had answered: "You weren't there, Mina. You were nowhere."

"Of course I was here, Eli, don't be silly," she'd said impatiently. "And so were you. Here, exactly where you are now."

"I'm here now," Eli answered quietly, "but before, I was nowhere."

"When are we going home?" Eli asked now. Mina hugged the thin little body to her. Only five years younger, and so small.

"We're not going home, Eli. I explained to you. We're going to America. To see Papa. Do you remember the map? All the blue, that's the water, the ocean. And we're going in a boat, a huge boat, across the ocean to America, a very lovely place, full of toys and big buildings . . . don't you remember me telling you? Showing you?"

Eli smiled. "I remember the map." He raised his left hand. "America's on that page. Very big. Next to all the blue."

"That's right." Mina laughed. "We're going right across the blue, and when we reach America, Papa will meet us."

"Can I take my horse out now?"

"Soon. It's in the suitcase. Soon we'll be on the boat, and you can take it out."

"Is it all right, in that suitcase?"

"Of course it is."

"I wish I could hold it," Eli whispered.

"Soon," Mina said. "As soon as we're on the sea. Now come and find Mama."

Eli worried about his horse. Could he see anything, shut in a dark suitcase? There were silver candlesticks in there, and tablecloths, and even pillows. Perhaps the horse will lie on the pillows and sleep, thought Eli. If you close your eyes, there's darkness everywhere, and it won't matter being shut up. He likes to roll about, though, on his wheels. Lovely green wheels. His black woolen tail swings from side to side. When Papa made him, ribbons of wood curled all over the floor. If the fat boy knew I had a horse painted red, with a long, black tail, he would take it.

Mina won't let him. One day, they tried to take him. On the way home from school, the first day. Mina fetched me. They shouted at us: "Jews! Jews! There's a ginger Jew!" and "Gingerhead!" and she ran at all the boys, and kicked them and bit them and pulled their hats off, and one of the boys took the horse and stamped on him and broke all the wheels off, and I was crying, I couldn't see, and Mina had blood all over her face. It was running down her face in lines, and her hair was messy and her dress was torn, and she picked the horse up out of the mud and pulled me all the way home, and I couldn't see because I was crying so much, and I kept falling over, and Mama washed all the blood away from Mina's face and Papa made new wheels for the horse, and painted his legs where he was scratched, but next day, I left the horse at home.

I thought the boys would leave us alone, but they always shouted, every day. Sometimes they threw stones, but Mina threw them back, and so they stopped, and just made faces and shouted. I see the faces at night, sometimes, all twisted up and pulled out of shape, like masks, and I wake up crying. I can't tell anyone how horrible they are. In America, Mina says, no one will shout at us, but I don't believe it. That horrible woman called her "Carrot-top!" Everybody has a face that can twist out of shape.

Rain was falling, pricking like needles into the dark surface of the water. The dockside buildings were tiny now, far away, nearly out of sight. If you looked the other way there was nothing but sea, miles and miles of empty ocean lying deep under the ship, which had loomed so high above their heads as they stood on the quay: the mighty *S.S. Danzig*. Now she seemed as fragile as the walnut shells that Eli used to float across the puddles. Almost everyone had wept as the ship left. Not me, though, thought Mina. Why should I weep if I'm going to a better place? In America, there will be paper, thick and white, and every kind of pencil, and paints in pots, all the colors there are, gloppy and shiny like mayonnaise. In America, I will go to school and learn to speak English, and people will be more polite, and I won't have my hair pulled and no one will call me names or laugh at Eli. In America, no one will hate us, or kill us, or set our houses on fire. Mama will have a piano again. I will ride in streetcars and look at tall buildings, wide streets, and shops full of everything.

Eli was leaning over the railing.

"Be careful, Eli," Mina said. "Don't fall in."

"How far down does it go, Mina?"

"I don't know. A long way down."

"I know, a long, long way. And in there are all kinds of things: dead ships and sea serpents and huge fishes that can eat you."

Mina shivered. "Shall I take you down? Mama's there. We could find your horse. You'll be warmer."

"It's horrible there. It smells. There are too many people." That was true. Golda and her baby were there, and Rachel and her father, and the horrible woman with her horrible son, and others, many, many others. People lying on bunks, all pushed up next to one another like loaves of bread on a bakery shelf, sitting on the floor, on suitcases, on old blankets, peering at each other in the yellowish light. There was no air. Smells of bread and herrings and tobacco smoke and damp clothes and garlic and unwashed bodies hung like clouds in the room. You could almost put out your hand and touch them. Hannah had been filled with dismay.

"How will we live like this? For two weeks. No privacy, like animals. Worse than animals. What will become of us?"

"We'll live like everybody else. We'll manage,"

Mina said, smiling bravely. "We get food, after all. It won't be very good, of course, but we'll live at least. They aren't allowed to starve us. It doesn't matter to be dirty for a little while. We'll have hot baths with soft white towels when we get home."

"Home?"

"I mean to America."

"Please God we should reach America safely." Hannah sighed. "You and Eli will sleep up there. I can't climb so far. God knows what kind of sleep we'll have here. Do you hear the noise? Babies, old men, coughing, laughing, crying. It'll never stop."

"Come up on the deck. The air's fresh at least."

"No, I'll stay here. Who knows who anybody is? They can take all our belongings while our backs are turned. I'll stay here."

Eli was staring at the water. Mina ran her hands over the rough, damp paint of the railings.

"It isn't blue," said Eli. "The water . . . you said blue. I thought it would be pale blue like the sky . . . all the time."

Mina frowned. "I thought blue too, but dark like summer evenings. Maybe the blue comes later, maybe it's only like this when it's cold and rainy."

"What color is it now?"

"I don't know. Not gray, and not brown and not green, but all three. And dark. I didn't think it would be so dark. Perhaps it's a special color: sea color."

"Would you like a sugared almond?"

Mina looked up. An old lady was smiling at her.

"Yes. Thank you."

"And your brother? Is it your brother?"

"Yes, it is. Sugared almonds! Really, I can't believe it."

"Really," said the old lady. "I think that what we will miss on this voyage is luxuries. Luxuries are just as necessary as necessities. That's what I think."

Mina nodded, her mouth full of hard, pink, sugary splinters. She grinned.

"I always say to myself, I'll suck them and suck them very slowly until all the sugar is off and make it last as long as possible, and then I can't bear it and I just crunch it all up at once, because it's so delicious."

The old lady nodded and went back to sit on her suitcases. Leather suitcases, Mina noticed. Very old, and torn in places, but leather nevertheless. A fur hat and collar and gloves of kid, and under the gloves the shapes of rings on many fingers. She sat with her back very straight. She looks, Mina thought, like a countess. If I were drawing her, I would put a chandelier over her head. She would sit on a straight mahogany chair, with a seat covered in brocade. Perhaps she was a countess who had lost all her money, or why was she traveling like this? Or maybe she had her own cabin on one of the upper decks?

"Would you like to find your cabin?" Mina asked. "Eli and I could help you carry your suitcases. The ladders are so steep."

"Thank you, child," said the countess with dignity.

"I shall delay going down as long as possible. I am traveling steerage. You look amazed." She laughed. "You think I am a rich old woman, because of the fur and the rings, yes?"

Mina nodded.

"Luxuries. The fur and the rings and the leather suitcases and the sugared almonds are not symbols of what I possess. They are everything I have."

"I'm sorry," Mina said quietly.

"Don't be sorry. I refer only to material possessions. My name is Clara Zussmann, from Lemburg in Austria. I have my wits and my health and my ticket to America. There, I have my son and his wife and their children, and also the children of my other son, may God rest him. They have sent for me. There is nothing left in the old country to keep me from coming." She smiled at Mina. "Who is that boy talking to your brother? I've noticed him before. Do you know him?"

Mina turned. "No, but thank you for the sugared almonds. I'd better go and see if Eli's all right. I have to look after him, you see. He's only nine, and he's a little nervous."

"Of course, child . . . of course." Mrs. Zussmann nodded. "I am sure we will see one another in the Winter Palace."

"Winter Palace?"

"I mean down there." She pointed. "That's what I call it. If you call something by a grand name, it can only make things better. It's funny, if nothing else."

"I suppose so," said Mina. "I must go now. Goodbye." She waved and turned to the railing again. Eli had his listening look on: eyes wide and mouth hanging open.

Mina ignored the boy who was talking to him and said, "Are you all right, Eli? What is he telling you?"

"Oh, Mina, wonderful things! Imagine, he's going to a place where there are high mountains and sunshine all the time and oranges growing on trees, so that you can pick them . . . and flowers. Not America."

"How can you not be going to America?" Mina looked at the boy.

"It is America, but not New York. I am going to go right across America to the West. California. It's warm there."

"And what will you do there?"

"I'll be a farmer."

Mina laughed. "How can you be a farmer? You mean your father will be a farmer."

"No, me. My father is dead, and my mother. I lived with my grandmother. My uncle sent a ticket. He's in New York, but I'm not staying there."

"Will your uncle let you go?"

"I'll run away," said the boy. "Anyway, with five children of his own, how sorry will he be to see me go? My uncle, I mean."

Mina looked at him. He was dark-haired and pale and only a little taller than she was.

"What's your name?" she asked.

"Daniel Bergman."

"I'm Mina Isaacs. This is my brother Eli."

"I know. I saw you before, kicking that boy."

"He deserved it. He said Eli was mad. I'm glad I kicked him. You think I shouldn't have done it, I suppose."

"I never said you shouldn't. I think kicking Yankel Katz is a very good idea. I wish I could have kicked him, too."

"You know him?" Mina grinned.

"And his mother. They lived near my grandparents."

"Are they are horrible as they look?"

"Worse!"

Mina started laughing, and the laughter grew and grew until tears poured from her eyes and she had to hold on to the railings to steady herself. Daniel and Eli laughed, too.

"I don't know what I'm laughing about," Daniel said finally.

Mina dried her eyes and tried to speak.

"I don't know . . . it's so funny . . . you said they're worse than they look . . . and they look so terrible, I thought, how can anybody be worse than that, worse than how they look? Don't you see?"

"I don't understand," said Eli.

"It's all right, Eli," said Mina, bursts of laughter still bubbling up inside her. "It's not really funny. You keep away from that Yankel that's all."

"Next time he does something I'll help you kick him," said Daniel.

"Who needs help? I can deal with him myself,

thank you very much," said Mina.

"Can't we take turns?" Daniel was smiling. "Why should you have all the fun?"

They burst out laughing all over again.

Mina

The clouds along the horizon look like mountains, but not mountains with sharp edges. Piled up, like dark blue wool, and above them the sky is pale. Maybe tomorrow I can see the sun go down into the water and the sky will be red and orange and the sea—who knows what will happen to the sea? It changes every minute and there's no end to it. Puddles, ponds, even the river at home you could see the end of, you could look at the opposite bank and say: I will swim, or walk, or jump over this water until I get to the other side. But this is different. How do I know that the other side is there? It's like flying up and up into the sky and never coming down at all, just floating forever in space. But Papa is in America, so it must be there, and I'm a fool. The map would never lie. Millions of people travel on the sea all the time. Sailors, fishermen. There have always been sailors, many sailors and many ships from all the harbors of the world. Where are they, then? Where, in all this ocean, is one tiny little ship for me to see? Just one, so that I know we are not alone. Alone, and going nowhere.

Chapter 2

RACHEL COULDN'T SLEEP. THE THROBBING OF THE ENGINES just below them, the creaking of old wood as the ship rolled over the water, snores, muffled tears and sniffs, crying children—they stopped her from sleeping. Some people slept: Mina, with her long red hair hanging over the edge of the bunk; that nice, gentle Mr. Kaminsky, who, it was whispered, had survived the terrible pogrom in Kishinev, and who was setting out for America with a sack full of books and very little else; even Golda. And more surprisingly, even Golda's baby. Rachel stared at the boards of the bunk above her. She couldn't see if her father was asleep. Did he dream dreams? I am frightened of my dreams, Rachel thought. I don't want to sleep because I am frightened of what I might see. She had told Golda about the dreams.

Golda had said. "But you see those things, you remember them all the time, even when you're awake. You must be quite used to them by now. Why don't you at least sleep a little while you think of them?"

"They're worse in the dreams," Rachel had answered. "Everything is worse in the dreams."

"What you need"—Golda spoke almost crossly—"is something new to dream about. Someone new. Look about you. The world is full of people. Isn't there one that you could love a little?" Not even one?"

"One day. Maybe . . ." Rachel had muttered.

"One day!" Golda laughed. "And you think he will rise up in front of you like an angel sent from Heaven, and say, 'Rachel, Rachel, I am the right one for you!' You're too romantic. You must look a little, seek out someone, talk to him, get to know him, and then quite naturally . . ."

"I can't talk, just like that. What could I say? I have nothing to say."

Golda had looked amazed. Who could have nothing to say? To her, all the hours of the day were not long enough for the words just longing to jump out of her mouth.

"So dream!" She had said, exasperated. "Why should I worry? Dream all you want, but don't blame me if you get pale and pinched so that in the end no one will want you. But Rachel, listen, on this boat there will be many young men—have you seen them? All handsome and strong and ready to start a new life. Have you seen them all?"

"To you, Golda, any man who hasn't got a hunch-back and warts on his nose is handsome and strong, and any man who is less than a hundred years old is young." Rachel had laughed.

"I'm an optimist. I think positively. That's good, not bad. You shouldn't be so fussy. And you can laugh, but I'll tell you something. Men become more handsome as you get to know them. My Moishe is not an oil painting, I promise you; but because I love him, that makes him handsome, don't you see?"

"Oh, Golda, of course I see. Do you think I am a fool? Who could live with an oil painting, anyway? I'm just . . . not ready, that's all."

"And when will you be ready? Perhaps when the Messiah comes?" Golda had sighed and rocked the baby, muttering under her breath.

Rachel closed her eyes. Tonight, please, let me dream of something good. Let me dream of my mother before she became ill, before the coughing filled the dark hours. How she looked when I was small, holding my hand in the street, laughing with the woman who sold chickens. Strong, carrying me home on one hip because I was tired and holding a basket full of apples and car-rots and potatoes and cabbages on the other. I can't see her like that for more than a moment. I can't hold good pictures in my mind. Only pillows behind her head, bones sticking out almost from under her skin, and coughing and coughing, and the sour smell of illness, and saying goodbye, leaving her lying there. Walking out of the door, out of the house and into the wagon and crying and not daring to look back, knowing, feeling that she would be weeping, too, with all the old women around her to comfort her and tell her lies. It would only be a short time. She would get better, she would follow us to America, we would prepare a place for her. It was only a matter of time.

Mother knew they were lies, and she pretended to believe them, because she knew that I would not leave her all alone, if I thought she was dying. The tears were falling from Rachel's eyes and she brushed them away. But I did know, she thought. Of course I knew. But I couldn't stay, because if I stayed then she would know that I knew she was dying, and that she couldn't bear. Wasn't her whole life one long struggle to guard me, to shield me, to protect me from the bad things, from hunger, from darkness, from danger? Rachel tossed her head from side to side. Perhaps I should have stayed with her, even though it made her unhappy? Like this, I will never see her again. I know it. She knew it. Father believes in miracles—or says he does. Who knows what dreams he is dreaming up there?

The dream about Mother, that was one dream. Just a long black tunnel, growing longer and blacker, and walking along the tunnel into the dark, and her small white face at the other end shrinking and shrinking and finally being swallowed up in the surrounding night. And the dark wasn't empty. It was full of noises: talk and laughter and snatches of song that could never wipe out a distant sound of weeping that grew louder and louder until it filled everything, every corner of the space all around.

Rachel turned to face the wall. Was it called a wall on a ship? During the day it seemed solid enough, studded with metal rivets, but now at night it was like a thin skin stretched between herself and the moving water all around. Just so must the egg feel in its shell, she thought. Please, please don't let me dream the beautiful dream tonight, don't let me even think of it. Any nightmare, any terror, anything, is better than that, better than waking up in the morning and knowing that it *was* only a dream, that it is no longer true, that it never will be true. Please don't let me dream that Chaim is alive again.

There wasn't much space to walk up and down. One, two, three, four and you bumped into a huge suitcase; one, two, three, four in another direction and there was a bunk. Golda held her baby close and swayed gently from side to side, trying to rock her to sleep. At least she had stopped crying, that was something. It will be morning soon, thought Golda. If it isn't raining, I will take her on the deck for some air. If it isn't too windy or too cold. My poor little bird, my Sarah, breathing in this terrible smell. In America, the rooms will smell of flowers. I'll have a vase on the sideboard, maybe cut glass. Maybe one day even crystal. And lace curtains, and a beautiful cradle for the baby with soft blankets for winter. Who is snoring like that? Up and down the scale, complete with crescendos and trills and long, vibrating diminuendos? Mr. Kaminsky? No, he is snuffling quite quietly. Probably Mr. Klein. Rachel is sleeping and, please God, not dreaming. She looks peaceful enough, even smiling a little. Golda looked around trying to find the source of the musical snoring. There he is, she thought. That fat man, there. He could live off that stomach for the whole two weeks. Suddenly, someone cried out. A cry of pain.

"Oh, I'm sorry," Golda whispered, kneeling down. "I think I trod on your hand. I'm so sorry. Oh, it's you."

A young man smiled at her.

"What do you mean, it's me? Do you know me?"

"Well," said Golda, "I've seen you, of course. On the deck, I think, as we were sailing." And remembered you, she thought, because you are so tall and handsome and seem so happy. Because you do not seem to be thinking all the time about what you are leaving behind.

"And I," said the young man, "have seen you and remembered you. Such beauty is rare, such elegance."

Golda smiled. "You mustn't talk to me like that. I'm a married woman. With a child."

"So who shall I talk to . . . like that, as you put it?"

Golda said, "I will introduce you to my friend Rachel Klein."

The young man frowned. "The one you were talking to in the shed?"

Golda blushed. He really has noticed me, she thought.

"Yes, a lovely girl. Really, you'll like her."

"I'm sure she's delightful. She must be, of course, if she's your friend, but she's . . . not my type."

"Your type? How do you know what's your type?"

"I know you are."

"Hush!" Golda put a finger to her lips. "If you speak like that, I won't talk to you. Rachel is beautiful."

"She's pale and skinny and looks as if she hasn't two words to rub together. You'll excuse me for being frank."

"What's your name?" asked Golda.

"Yasha Dubowsky," said the young man. "And you are Golda Schwartz."

"Who told you?"

"I listen, that's all."

Golda giggled. "The baby is waking up again. I must walk a little. Tomorrow, I'll introduce you to Rachel."

Yasha took a postcard from the inside pocket of his jacket and held it up to catch what light there was. It was a little creased, a little dog-eared, there was even a small stain in one corner, but still . . . but still. His cousin had sent it to him from Paris. It was a picture of the most beautiful woman he had ever seen, sitting on a swing whose ropes were twined with flowers. Her face shone out like a star from under her feathered hat. Her skirts were drawn up nearly to her knees, and in among her foamy petticoats you could actually see her legs, silky and white, and her feet in shiny white boots. Yasha had never seen a real woman's legs, had never guessed that they would be like this, was quite sure, indeed, that they wouldn't. How could Naomi's legs ever peep out from clouds of petticoats? He imagined them as almost like his own: strong, solid parts of the body designed to work, to carry her around as she fed the chickens and walked to the market through muddy roads that spattered her heavy shoes.

In America, there would be women like the postcard lady. Not sitting on flowery swings, of course, and showing their ankles. Yasha laughed. Even I am not such a mad dreamer as to imagine that. But, he thought, there, there would be elegance, wealth, beautiful clothes, and real women who might easily wear such a froth of petticoats beneath their skirts, and they will all come to me, to my shop, because I will no longer be bent over the rusted innards of Reb Finkel's antique watch with a glass in my eye, oh no. I will own a jewelry shop filled with treasures. Rings and brooches and chains, diamonds and sapphires, and emeralds, dainty gold wristwatches for the ladies and handsome fobs and hunters for the men. Others will do the repairs. I won't spend hours bending over a small desk in a back room. I will be in the front of the shop, finely dressed, bringing out trays of gems;

and the white hands of very rich ladies will twinkle in and out of all the jewels. How could Naomi ever have fitted in? She would have been miserable, Yasha assured himself. Better she should marry someone else, someone who can make her happy. I never chose her, he told himself. They chose her for me.

What he remembered most clearly about Naomi's house was the furniture. Here, on the ship, in the boxlike compartment, there were no chairs, sofas, chests of drawers, cupboards, sideboards, grandfather clocks, occasional tables, looking glasses, ornaments, figurines and china knickknacks. Perhaps that was why everyone sat huddled on the bunks. Bare boards are something no one likes. Home means furniture. In Naomi's house, the day the marriage was arranged, they all sat around a table covered with red plush. The dark, heavy backs of the chairs loomed up over their heads, carved into leaves and branches, like small, hard knots of forest. All around the walls, black cupboards towered like mountains. The floor was thickly carpeted. You couldn't hear anyone walking. Money: that was what all the furniture represented, and the gray silk of Naomi's mother's dress, her elaborate wig and the brooch at her throat, gathering up the edges of a real lace collar. Naomi's mother had too many teeth and a mouth that bunched up around them like a drawstring bag pulled tightly shut. When she smiled, it was as though someone had loosened the string. She seldom smiled, which was perhaps fortunate.

Yasha had tried to feel love for Naomi. He had

tried hard. At least a glimmering, a surge of feeling, sympathy, something. His father had said, "Love? What is love? Love grows. Love is nothing to begin with, a tiny seed, perhaps, but it flowers with time. Knowledge is love. Working and living together is love, sharing a life. That's what love is. The love we read about in books, my boy, is something else. Maybe sometimes you find it in your life, but most people do not. Marriage is like a good plot of ground for love. It can grow there from the smallest beginnings, grow and flourish." But flourish into what, Yasha had thought, flourish into a cauliflower or a potato? Nourishing, yes, and good and worthy, but not a flower. Not beautiful and fragrant and sweet enough to make you dizzy. Looking at Naomi, Yasha knew he could never love her. All the soft carpets and silver trays in the world could not make him love her. He felt two things. Two voices were whispering in his mind all the time. One voice said: so what does it matter? She is good, she is rich, you will want for nothing. There will be food and children and work, what more could anyone want? And another voice said: You will never love her, you will sink here into a featherbed of a life without having seen anything, done anything, gone anywhere. Without having felt any emotions at all, not anger, not passion, not despair, nothing.

His parents were discussing the wedding. They would give this, and Naomi's parents would provide that. So many feather quilts and sheets (hand embroidered) and tables and chairs and coffeepot and samovar and spoons and knives and carpets and linen and glasses and cooking pots and pans and wardrobes; as they spoke about them, Yasha could almost see them piled up on the table in front of him, hiding Naomi from him, hiding and overshadowing them both. She didn't say a word. She didn't look happy. Her face was the color of uncooked bread. The room was hot, and he felt his collar (clean and starched for the occasion) biting into the flesh of his neck. Run away, said the voice in his head. Now, before it is too late. Run. Run. But where to? Where can I go? And then the answer came: to America. I will sell the gold watch that grandfather left me, Yasha decided, and run to America. He took the watch out of his waistcoat pocket and looked at it, and as he looked, the room and the furniture and Naomi and her parents and his own parents and all the talk, talk, talk about dowries and weddings slipped further and further away, until he felt distant from all of it, as though he were looking at it from the wrong end of a very long telescope.

Yasha turned over in his bunk. Now, he thought, I've done it. I've left her and run away. From her, and from a life where the biggest excitement is a trip to Minsk once or twice a year. America, he thought. America is the place for me. There, a person can do something, be someone, make a proper life. Visions of carriages and white shirt-fronts, of lighted shop windows and tall buildings filled his brain as he put the postcard away again. He thought of what Golda had said, and smiled. Rachel Klein was still sleeping. She was prettier than Naomi, but a long, long way from the girl on the swing.

A wide room with polished floors and chandeliers and a small orchestra playing "The Blue Danube." Red wine sparkling in glasses with long, transparent stems, and feet in satin slippers, dancing round and round until you felt giddy from the movement. Clara Zussmann opened her eyes and blinked and shook her head. Only a dream, after all, but so lovely. The movement was real, though, backwards and forwards as the ship rolled. It was not unpleasant.

Clara thought, I had expected it to be worse than this. I should wash my face, she told herself, I should try and keep at least a little clean. Then she remembered the ten grubby basins, used by all of them, used for everything, even washing dishes, and she shuddered.

She sat up and took a small bottle of eau de cologne from her bag and dabbed a little on her temples. For a moment, its fragrance covered all the other smells, but after a while it was absorbed into the heavy air, gone forever.

Clara lay back. For breakfast now, she thought, fresh rolls with honey and hot coffee from the silver coffeepot. She smiled. How long had it been since that coffeepot had been on the table? Years. When Isaac died, everything had been sold, and at stupid prices, to buy tickets for the boys to go to America. Much good had it done them! Poor Asa, dead from tuberculosis within a year from the steam of the iron in the pressing shop and not enough to eat, and his wife Miriam dead too, six months ago, from grief or illness, or both together, who knew? And their children, no more than babies, living now with David and Rebecca and their children, so that Rebecca had to work, too, to feed them all. Clara sighed. She knew the kind of work it was. She had read their letters, both what they wrote and what they left out. Rebecca would be sewing, sewing with a machine, clothes for women who would not think for an instant of the strained eyes and hurting back and pricked fingers of the one who made them. A golden land, a land of opportunity, a land of poverty and misery and hard work. My grandchildren should eat roasted meat with beans in a sauce like dark red velvet, fried fish and soup with dumplings in it. Years ago, that is what they would have eaten. They think, David maybe thinks, that if I come, I will be able to make it the same as it was. He doesn't say so, but what child, even one that has grown into a man, doesn't expect his mother to feed him, to look after him as she used to, and if not him, then his children? And how will I be able to? Is it any wonder I bring sugared almonds and eau de cologne in my luggage? Who can blame me? The days of boiled cabbage will soon be upon me, boiled cabbage in a cold room. Clara closed her eyes. Better not to think of such things.

Hannah Isaacs felt sick. The movement of the ship, the smell (had someone vomited in the night?), the stuffy heat, filled her with such nausea that she could not raise her head from the pillow. I'm delicate, she thought. I've always been like that, like Eli. He takes after me. He's delicate too. Sensitive. Imaginative. Shy. And Mina? Who knows who Mina takes after? Hannah thanked God aloud every day for her strong and energetic daughter, who had always known, from when she was a young child, it seemed, how to clean, how to cook, how to look after Eli. Such a help. Privately Hannah wished that she were not so skinny, that her hair were not quite so red, that she spoke less, and less sharply, that she were more . . . Hannah searched for a suitable word . . . girlish. I would have taught her to play the piano, if she had shown the slightest interest. So pleasant, a pretty young lady playing the piano. What good will her drawing do her, fingers black with charcoal, dress covered in paint? What man will want her? If she is not drawing, her head is stuck in a book. What good will it do? Hannah couldn't bear to think about it, so she thought instead of her piano. The day they sold it to help pay for the tickets, the day it was carried out of the house, Hannah cried as though a dear friend had died, as though the men had carried a coffin through the door. The silence after it had gone oppressed her. Mina had drawn a picture for her of the piano they would have in America, with candle holders and a plush seat that opened so that you could keep your music inside. Mina. Such a good girl really, and I love her so much. Why is it I find it hard to show her, sometimes?

Mina woke up before Eli. His feet were right next to her face. She turned away. Mama was sighing. It's hard to breathe in here, Mina thought. I shall go up to the deck and see what the day is like. I shall wake Eli up and take him, too. She sat up and looked around. The fat Katz boy was also sitting up, eating an orange. He frowned at her and thumbed his nose. Mina stuck her tongue out, but he had turned away and did not see. Stupid boy, she thought, and looked at Eli.

In a tiny part of her mind, a thought stirred: What if he is right, that boy? What if they do send Eli back? He isn't like other people.

Nonsense, she told herself. How will they know? He won't have to speak. I'll speak for him, and in any case, not in English. They won't know what he's saying in Yiddish. They won't pay any attention to such a small child among all these people. But what, whispered an inward voice, what if they have clever American doctors who can see right into you and read your thoughts, what then? An image suddenly filled her mind of Eli's face watching her from the railings of a huge black ship, growing smaller and smaller as she stood on the dockside and watched her brother being carried away. Where? To whom? How could he go back all alone? Who would be so cruel? Who could look after him? For a moment, Mina sat transfixed by a terror so great that it filled every corner of her body, but then the moment passed. It would be all right. Eli would be let in. He wasn't mad. No one could say that he was mad. To be frightened about such a thing would be like admitting he was crazy. I won't be frightened. I refuse to be frightened. As she shook Eli awake, she thought, I'll ask Daniel what the regulations are. Maybe there isn't any such rule. Why should I believe the Katz family? And, if Eli is sent back, then I shall go with him, and no one will be able to stop me.

"Eli," she said. "Wake up. Let's go and see what color the sea is."

Eli

When I throw a stone into a puddle, it sinks into the mud. When I throw a stone into the river behind the orchard, it is gone. It goes down and down through the water. Sometimes you can see it if the water is clear, going down and down until it lies on top of all the other stones that are there. Stones sink and leave circles on the top of the water. Things that float on water are leaves, feathers, egg shells, light things. This ship is made of wood and iron. Wood can be light, but not iron. And there are people. Many people. Some of them must be heavy. And suitcases and trunks and bundles. Our suitcase is so heavy I can't lift it. I don't understand why this heavy ship doesn't fall through the water, all the miles and miles of water, and lie at the bottom of the sea like a huge rock. How does it sit on the waves and roll around and never topple over and not sink? How? And where are all the fishes that are supposed to be in the sea? When will we catch sight of them? The sky is blue today, with wispy clouds like hair, but the sea is still dark. Shiny in the sun so that you can't look for very long, but not blue. Mina says maybe, but I don't think this sea will ever be blue. Not ever.

Chapter 3

YANKEL KATZ WAS BORED.

"I haven't got anything to do," he said to his mother.

"And I have plenty, I suppose. Card games and tea parties and pleasure of every kind. What do you think this ship is, a fun fair?"

"But what can I do all the time?" A whining note had crept into Yankel's voice.

"Look at the sea."

"I looked at it already."

"Maybe it looks different today. Maybe today there'll be mermaids . . ."

"It's never different. How can it be different? It's water."

Mrs. Katz sighed. "Then go and talk to somebody."

"I don't like anybody."

"What about Daniel?"

"He won't talk to me. He's fifteen. Anyway, he's always with Mina and that stupid Eli."

"Then read a book."

"I haven't got a book."

"Ask Mr. Kaminsky. He has every book you could wish for."

"They're boring. Not storybooks."

"How do you know? Have you asked? Suddenly you have eyes that can see inside the covers of books without even opening them."

Yankel was silent. There was nothing to do and that was that. Not even the fun of tormenting Eli. Normally, Yankel would have quite enjoyed teasing him or frightening him, because Eli had eyes that quickly filled with tears and couldn't or wouldn't fight back, but that was out of the question now because of Mina, who, surprisingly, didn't seem to be scared of him at all, and Daniel, who was too big to bully. But I'd like, Yankel thought, to pay Mina back for that kick. He thought for a few moments about how to do this, but no brilliant ideas occurred to him.

"I'm hungry," he said to his mother.

"And everyone else is full, I suppose," she snapped back. "Eating dry bread and bits of this and that and the swill they give us in those pails. For thirty-three dollars, you'd think they could provide food a person could eat, but no. Animal slops. I'll starve to death before I touch it. Thank God I feel too seasick to be hungry. Go and look at the sea. Maybe there's a storm. Who knows. Maybe we'll all be shipwrecked and drowned before we ever reach America."

"I don't want to," said Yankel. "I hate this ship. I hate everyone on her." He lay on his bunk, preparing to sulk the day away.

"Tsk! Tsk!" murmured Mrs. Katz, almost to herself. "What have I done to deserve such a dissatisfied child?"

"And this," said Mina, her pencil flying over the paper spread out between them on the deck, "is Reb Chernowsky, standing in the door of the schoolhouse with his stick, ready to hit lazy children."

"Did he really have eyebrows like that?" Daniel laughed.

"Worse," said Mina. "I'm flattering him. They were like bushes, and bushes used to grow out of his nostrils, too." She filled them in with feathery strokes.

Eli said, "Draw the house. Draw our street."

Mina drew. Wooden houses, some with two stories, some more like huts, wooden shops, and the synagogue at the end of the road.

Eli said, "I wish I could walk into the picture and into our house."

"It may not be like that now, Eli," Mina said gently. "Do you remember what they did to the Wolffs' house?"

"Yes," Eli said. "Don't draw that, Mina."

"No," said Mina. "No, I never would."

We were the only ones who saw what really happened to the Wolffs' house, Eli and me, thought Mina. I told Mama about it, much later, when it was nearly forgotten. I was frightened to speak of it before, because if they, the ones who did it, had known we were watching, they would have killed us both, just like a slaughterer kills chickens. I knew that. It all started with Eli. He was missing again. He had wandered off, and I had to find him. After looking all over the village, I saw him behind a herring barrel in the market. It was dark and everyone had gone home. Black night everywhere, except for squares of yellow light shining from the windows of lamp-lit rooms.

"We must go home now, Eli," I said. "Do you know what time it is?"

"I don't want to walk in the dark. I'm afraid."

"What of? Now, come on, hold my hand and count the windows all along the street. Look, there's the Wolffs' house. Isn't it grand? Did Mama tell you about the inside? She went there once. Come, walk with me, and I'll tell you."

We picked our way slowly along the street. It was so dark that we could hardly see our feet. Suddenly, out of the darkness, I heard the sound of horses hooves pounding on the hard road and the noise of laughter. I don't know why, to this day I don't know why, because I can't remember thinking: *this* is what you must do; all I remember is grabbing Eli by the hand and pulling him down behind a flap of canvas that hung from the front of one of the stalls.

"Don't move," I whispered. "Don't say a word. Stay very still, like a mouse."

The sound of the horses came nearer and nearer. They drummed with their hooves on the earth beside our stall, and the canvas shook. There were four men, carrying huge torches that lit up the darkness with scarlet and gold.

"What will they do?" Eli whispered.

"Ssh! I don't know. They've stopped outside the Wolffs' house."

We peered round the canvas. The horses pawed the ground outside the big wooden house. Glass cracked and broke and split open the silence. Two flaming torches whistled through the air and into the broken window. Another curved like a comet and landed on the roof. The horsemen galloped past us again, vanishing like black shadows into the darkness. Smoke began to puff out of the cracks between the wooden boards of the house. We heard shouting. Screaming, as the Wolffs ran out into the street. Someone was throwing furniture and bedding from an upstairs window. Chairs covered with velvet lay upside down in the dust. The children were crying. Pnina Wolff was sobbing. The house was alight, shining and crackling with flames that seemed to touch the sky. Columns of smoke stretched out of the roof and clouded the whole street. The neighbors had come to help. Pnina and the children were led away. Moses Wolff stood in the road like a statue, watching the house burn.

"We're going home, Eli," I said. "Quick. And don't say a word to anyone."

"Why?"

"Why? Are you a baby? If those men find out that we were watching, that we saw them, they'll . . ."

"What?"

"Nothing. They'll be very angry."

"Perhaps they'll set our house on fire. Do you think they will?"

I did think that, but all I said was, "Don't waste time. Run. And don't say a word."

We ran all the way to the other side of the village where we lived. By noon the next day, everyone knew about the Wolffs. Everyone went to see them with something: food or a piece of old furniture. They would have to start again. One of the seven children, the baby, died in the fire. Pnina Wolff didn't talk to anyone properly after that. She dressed in black and sang to herself all the time, even when people were talking to her. It was after the Wolffs' house was burned down that Papa left for America. Eli dreamed of black horses and men with faces that he couldn't properly see.

"I'm going to draw California," said Mina.

Daniel laughed. "But you've never been there."

"Neither have you," she answered, "but you know what it's like. You told me." She drew a long row of trees and mountains in the background. "I wish I had colors. Who can tell these are oranges? They look like lumps of coal. But look, this is you, Daniel, on a horse."

Daniel said, "The horse is good, but that doesn't look like me, really." He pointed at the figure of the rider.

Mina frowned, and stared at Daniel's pleasant, ordinary face. Perhaps the boy in her drawing was a little too handsome, a little too tall, like a prince.

She said, "Maybe not. It doesn't really matter."

Later, looking at the drawing by herself, she thought: this is how I think of him when his face is not in front of my eyes. It isn't the drawing that's wrong, only it's not a picture of Daniel, but of how I feel about him, because I like him, because he is the only boy I have ever met who doesn't speak to me as if I were a girl, a kind of pet that needs special attention and a different kind of conversation. He talks to me as if I were another person just like himself.

Abraham Klein had fallen into the habit of taking his midday bowl of thin, greasy soup and eating it beside Mr. Kaminsky. This was in part because Mr. Kaminsky looked so frail and sad, his mouth almost hidden by a white moustache, his hair standing up in small tufts above his ears. Also, it was because Mr. Kaminsky was clearly a learned man. Was he not always reading? It was always good to talk to a learned man. And of course, Abraham Klein was lonely. Rachel seemed to disappear whenever he wanted her. Where was she now, for instance? Up on that slippery deck, getting blown around like washing on a line. For his part, Abraham had no desire to see the sea. If he could forget that it was there for an hour or two, why then, those were happy hours. But it was difficult. If the ship were not pitching and rolling like some drunken peasant, then it creaked and moaned in the wind, and always, through every human smell, you could perceive a bitter whiff of salt, as though the very timbers had been pickled. Abraham said, "Are you not eating your soup today, Mr. Kaminsky?"

"Soup?" Mr. Kaminsky smiled. "I think they use the same straw to make it as they put in the pillows."

"Still, to keep up your strength . . ."

"That soup, if eaten regularly," said Mr. Kaminsky, "would fell an ox, my friend. A body is better off without it."

"If only they would let me into the kitchen here." Abraham sighed. "Did you know I used to be a baker? Soft rolls, with poppy seeds, and bread, every kind you can think of, and cakes with butter and cinnamon and raisins and apples and chocolate—"

"Mr. Klein, stop! I will weep. A baker. Well." Mr. Kaminsky considered. "In America, of course, you will have no difficulty in finding work. Why, think of it like this: in a few weeks, when you are buried in dough all night to make bread for the morning, you will say, 'Ah, how I wish I were back on the good old *Danzig*, peacefully talking with Mr. Kaminsky and eating straw soup.' "

Abraham laughed. "Perhaps, perhaps. We are never satisfied. But I hope to work, yes. A friend of my wife's cousin, he will put me in touch with all the bakers, of that I am sure. He is not a baker himself, of course. He deals in furs, animal furs for coats." Abraham paused. "However, I'm sure I shall find work. People will always need bread, thank God. And, naturally, I am hoping for a good marriage for Rachel."

"She is a lovely girl," said Mr. Kaminsky.

"Yes, yes, she will be a comfort to me in my old age," said Abraham. "The friend has a son, you see, and I haven't said anything to Rachel yet, but he is of the right age and a good family, and we have been in correspondence . . . It is not arranged, not formally, but we have . . . an understanding."

"An understanding that Rachel will marry this boy?" Mr. Kaminsky chuckled. "Ah, my friend, this is America we are going to. This is the twentieth century. Young people are different now. That is what I hear."

"It's true. It's true. But Rachel . . . well, she has

always been a devoted child."

"And you have not told her of this plan?"

"No." Abraham finished his soup. "There will be time enough for that when we arrive. Besides, she is still recovering from the death of a young man she loved very much. Back in the old country. It was a terrible thing . . . terrible. He was a learned young man, like yourself. In America, she will forget. She will be ready. Now, with the journey, and leaving her mother . . it's hard for a man to deal with a girl of Rachel's age, without a mother."

Mr. Kaminsky nodded. Abraham Klein sat silent, and the old man did not like to ask any more questions. Where was the mother? How did the young man die? I have looked at that Rachel, he thought. Her father does not know her. A skinny little thing, with sad eyes and pale hair, but strong, oh yes. A determined set to her mouth sometimes, and a brave smile. Please God she will love her cousin's friend's son, or whoever he is, because if she does not, Mr. Klein will find his plans in ruins. She is not the kind of person to submit in silence to anyone's wishes, and if she has been obedient and devoted up till now, it is because she has never wanted anything her parents did not also want for her. Mr. Kaminsky marveled that parents so often did not know their own children at all.

Rachel stood in the stern of the ship with her shawl
wrapped tightly around her shoulders and her long hair
blowing about her face. The wind flattened her thin
skirt against her legs and made it billow out in front of
her. The long white wake that the ship made in the dark
water fascinated her, and she watched new foam form-
ing into crests and peaks as the water closed over the
lines of white that stretched away behind them. A pale
sun was shining, but it gave no warmth. There were
clouds on the horizon.

"It's a marvelous sight, isn't it?" said a voice behind
her, and she turned, startled.

"Oh!" It was Yasha, the young man Golda talked
about incessantly. "I'm sorry. I was miles away. I didn't
see you."

"But I've been watching you." Yasha grinned.
"You looked very small there in all the wind."

Rachel gathered the flying strands of her hair together and pulled the shawl up over her head.

"I like the wind. It's very stuffy down in the compartment."

"I like it, too. I like the smell of salt and the sense
of freedom, and the feeling that the wind is blowing

away all the old, bad things, blowing us to a new life."

Rachel said nothing. This man was a talker, you could see that. Fond of the sound of his own voice. Quite pleased with himself, too, she thought, and who can blame him? For once Golda is right. He *is* young. And handsome. She tested herself for feelings. Do I like him? I don't know him. Will I be glad if he leaves me here and goes somewhere else? I wouldn't mind. Do I care what he thinks of me? Am I wondering if he thinks I am pretty? No, I'm not. She smiled to herself. Oh, Golda, I'm so sorry, she thought, love at first sight I haven't got.

"My name is Yasha Dubowsky," said the young man.

"I'm Rachel Klein."

"Delighted to meet you. If I were in New York, I would ask you to take tea with me, or dine. Unless"— he frowned—"you are already spoken for?" He smote his head with the flat of his hand. "What a fool I am! Of course you are already spoken for. There is a young man waiting in America to claim you as his bride, and nothing for me to do but throw myself into the sea!" He made as if to climb over the railings. Rachel pulled him back by his sleeve, laughing.

"What nonsense you talk! You're like a child. I'm not spoken for, as you put it, but even if I were, you hardly know me."

"At the moment, that's true. But I will know you very well by the end of the voyage."

"You are bored, that's all, and most of the young

women are married or betrothed. You've no one else to show off to."

Yasha was silent for a moment, and Rachel guessed she had been right. Then he smiled, and said, "Perhaps I was at first, but now . . . now I'm not so sure at all."

"It's perfectly all right," said Rachel. "There is no law that says you have to fall in love with me, you know. Golda has been matchmaking, hasn't she?"

Yasha blushed and smiled. "But we can be friends, can't we?" he said.

"Of course. Someone to talk to is always pleasant, but now you will excuse me. I have to go back to my father."

Yasha watched her go, steadying herself against the railings, head down, hiding from the wind. She looked so frail. Once, she nearly stumbled, and involuntarily, his hands stretched out to help her, to carry her, although she was many yards away. Yasha stood in the stern for a while, thinking of the strands of her hair blown like gold ribbons across her face, touched with chilly sunlight. He began to reach inside his jacket for the postcard of the girl on the swing, but then he let his arm fall to his side. Suddenly, he had no desire to look at that painted mouth and those silky legs; why, he did not know. The spell had always worked before. Could it be that Rachel . . . ? He laughed out loud. Never. That thin body dressed in gray, that pale face, with the mouth too wide . . . never. He remembered thinking, as she stood beside him, that he wanted very much to tuck her under his warm jacket and shelter her from the wind, but that was all. Nothing else. Probably he would have felt the same about anyone.

Rachel did not go and find her father. She climbed down to the dark, hot cavern where her bunk was, where she could hide.

"Are you feeling ill?" said Mina, noticing her lying there, looking at nothing.

"No. Thank you. Just tired. It's difficult to sleep here at night, isn't it?"

"I suppose so." Mina nodded. But she didn't understand. How should she. She was still young enough to be able to sleep.

"I'll just close my eyes for a moment," Rachel said.

"I'm sorry, of course you must. I'll let you rest."

Rachel smiled at her. "I'm not being unfriendly. You do know that, don't you?"

"Of course I do." Mina waved as she moved away. "I hope you sleep a little."

Rachel closed her eyes and thought of a field. Before she had met Chaim, it had been just a field. Quite pretty, with apple trees and plum trees growing along one side of it and a stream running through it. Just a field. She used to sit sometimes in the sun and take her stockings off and dabble her toes in the water. When the apples and plums were ripe, the pickers would wave to her from their ladders. She knew them all. One day, she had come to the stream, and someone was already there. A man. He was lying on his stomach, reading. Rachel felt as if her own private place had been invaded. He looked up as she approached and smiled at her.

"I can see by the look on your face that I shouldn't be here," said the man. "I'm sorry, I'll leave."

"No," said Rachel, confused because he was as young as she was, more a boy than a man, and because his eyes were the darkest she had ever seen. "It's all right, really. I'm only walking through . . . I'm going to see whether the apples are ready yet."

"Sit down for a moment. What's your name?"

"Rachel."

"My name is Chaim."

"You're not from here, are you?" said Rachel. "I've never seen you before."

"I'm from Kracow," said Chaim. "My grandparents live near here."

They talked, about everything, about nothing. They looked at one another. The sun was hot.

"Take your stockings off and dabble your toes in the stream," said Chaim later.

"No, no, I couldn't . . ."

"Why not?"

"You would see my legs . . ."

"And so?" said Chaim. "I have seen your arms and your neck and your face . . ."

"But legs . . ."

"Legs are only legs after all. Look." He took off his socks and shoes. "Here are mine."

Rachel blushed. "Very well, then. But turn away while I take my stockings off."

They dipped their toes into the cool water, laughing. The sun made gold flecks on the skin of their feet.

"Have you ever run barefoot across the grass?" Chaim asked.

"Yes, when I was little . . . I love to run, but I'm too old now."

"I'll race you to that tree," said Chaim. "Come on." He pulled her by the hand, and they ran and ran until they reached the tree. Rachel sank down into the shady grass. Chaim stood and looked at her.

"Will you tell me something, Rachel?"

"What is it?"

"Is there someone . . . anyone who—I mean, is your marriage already arranged?"

"No, no. I'm only sixteen. My mother needs me, and besides . . ."

"What?"

"I don't want a marriage arranged for me. I want to choose."

"I've chosen already."

"A girl from Kracow?"

"You."

"Me?"

"Yes." Chaim sat down beside her and looked at the grass. "I want to marry you."

"But you don't know me."

"That's true, but I love you. I love your toes."

Rachel laughed and hid her face in her skirts. "How can I tell my father that this man loves my toes and wants to marry me."

Chaim took her face between his hands. "It isn't only the toes. It's everything."

Rachel said, "Are you going to kiss me?"

"I don't know. Do you want me to?"

"I don't know. No one has ever kissed me before."

He put his mouth gently on her hair and kissed her. "There, like a brother, on your hair and your eyes . . ."

"No," said Rachel, not knowing herself, not recognizing who she was, or the feeling in her blood that made her say it, so strange was it, like a kind of drunkenness: "No, like this . . ." and she took his head and turned it so that his lips were on hers, and she threw her arms around him and felt his warmth against her and her head was spinning . . . She pushed him away and buried her face in her hands.

"Oh, I'm sorry, I'm sorry," she mumbled. "I don't know how I could behave . . . so . . . I don't know what happened to me. Will you forgive me? How can you forgive me?

"Will you marry me?" Chaim asked. Rachel nodded.

"Then tell me about your family, and I will tell you about mine, and from time to time I will kiss you, so be warned."

She lay against his shoulder under the tree. His arm was around her, and above them the leaves made a thick green canopy, latticed with brightness. It was an especially beautiful field from that day. The field where she met Chaim.

Yankel

*What is the point of being on a ship, on the sea, without
storms? It's boring. They said there would be gales,
with waves as high as houses crashing down on the
deck, and fogs so thick you couldn't see anything at all,
and all there's been is nothing. Rain and wind, that's
all, and you can get that on land, anyway. I'd like to
see a wave knock that stupid Mina off her feet. She
thinks she's so brave and clever. A real storm would
teach her. If there's a real storm, she'll be down there,
sick and crying with the rest of them: Eli and all those
old people, and I'll be up here, helping the sailors.
Perhaps I can catch hold of someone just before a wave
sweeps them overboard, and the captain will give me a
medal; and when we get to America, they'll put my
picture in all the newspapers. Then no one will laugh
at me any more. Not if I'm in the newspapers. Even
Daniel will be impressed. And Father. Mama says he
will be there to meet us. Perhaps he will be changed.
Maybe he'll be better now that he has some work to do.
If he isn't at home in the daytime, like he was, then
I'll only see him for a few hours in the evening. He'll
have to eat and wash and read the paper. He'll hardly
have time to shout at me at all.*

59

Chapter 4

"GOLDA?" SAID RACHEL, TRYING TO SPEAK OVER THE CRIES of the baby. "Golda? Are you crying? It's not like you to cry, you, so gay and happy always . . . what happened to make you cry?"

"Sarah . . ." Golda sobbed. "It's Sarah. She won't stop crying. I don't know what to do. I don't know if she's in pain, or sick, or maybe she's even dying, and I just don't know what to do."

"Let me take her for a minute," Rachel said. "How long has she been like this? Golda, you're exhausted. You must sleep, I'll look after Sarah." She took the baby and held her.

"She cried all night," said Golda. "I had to take her into the corridor and walk up and down all night. She fell asleep, after hours it seemed, and then I sat down on the floor to rest and she woke up again. I can't bear it. All night I had to move. The ship isn't enough for her, rolling from side to side. She needs me to roll as well . . . but Rachel, what's wrong with her? Will it ever stop? What are we going to do?"

Rachel held the small body so that it lay against her shoulder and closed her eyes. Another person, another human being, just like us, and we don't know anything, why she cries, what she needs. She could be a creature from the depths of the ocean, something strange and wonderful from another star . . . but mothers are supposed to know. Just like that. Know in their bones. Golda doesn't know. Sarah is crying, and Golda can't stop it, and her tiny face is all covered with tears and her hands clenching and unclenching. If only there was someone . . . a mother, someone older, someone who knew . . .

"Mina! Mina!" Rachel shouted across the compartment to where Mina and Daniel were talking. "Mina, go and find Mrs. Zussman. I don't know where she is . . . maybe on the deck . . . find her quickly and bring her . . . tell her Golda's baby won't stop crying. Tell her to come at once."

"Yes," said Mina. "I'll be back soon, don't worry. Eli, stay with Daniel." She was gone. The baby's cries grew louder, more urgent. Rachel looked at the red little face, more wrinkled than an old man's, the open mouth, the tiny fists clenched in, what? Rage, despair, pain? How to tell? Golda was twisting a handkerchief around and around in her fingers, unable to speak from tiredness.

Yankel Katz saw Eli rummaging in the suitcase and leaned out of his bunk for a better view. What was hidden in there? Food? He was taking a long time to find it. Ah, there it was. Something red . . . he was hiding it under his jacket. He doesn't want anyone to see it, thought Yankel, but I'll see it if it's the last thing I do. What's he doing with it? Going over to that baby who never stops crying. Taking it out and putting it on the mother's lap. It's a horse, that's all. That's what he was making such a fuss about and hiding like a piece of gold, a stupid, babyish, wooden horse. Just right for a stupid, babyish, crazy person like him.

"Here's my horse," said Eli.

"It's very nice, Eli," said Golda, "but not now. Please. My baby . . . I can't look at it properly now. Another time, perhaps, when the baby's asleep."

"But I brought it to show the baby. Maybe she'll stop crying . . . she can play with it if she likes . . ."

Rachel said gently, "Eli, it's a beautiful horse. Really. And thank you for bringing it. But the baby is too small. She can't hold it, her hands are too small. Probably she can hardly see it. She's like a tiny, tiny kitten. Just born. Do you understand?"

Eli tucked the horse under his jacket and turned to go.

"Eli," Rachel called him back. "It was very kind of you to bring the horse. Later, I would like to look at it. May I?"

"I suppose so," said Eli. "But I thought it would make the baby stop crying."

"I know, I know. But look, she's so small. Look at her. She's not much bigger than the horse, is she?"

"No. I'll go and put him back then. In the suitcase."

"Why don't you play with him? Wouldn't you like to play with him?"

"Yes. But it's safe in the suitcase." Eli went back to his mother's bunk and pushed the horse back into its place, making sure that it was lying on something soft.

Yankel Katz frowned. If I could get hold of that horse of his, that would be good; but the mother is always sick, always lying near the suitcase, and she would catch me. Why doesn't she get up, once in a while? Perhaps when she's using the lavatory . . . but that's not enough time . . . Yankel puzzled over the problem as he sat on the hard wooden floor next to his bunk, chewing a stale roll.

"Now . . . now . . ." said Clara Zussmann, sitting down next to Rachel. "Let me look at her." Rachel put the baby into her arms. Clara took no notice of Golda, nor of Rachel herself, but talked to the child, just as though it were a grown person, capable of understanding everything.

"What's the matter with you, then, madam? Don't you like this ship? Not enough luxury for you, is there?

Not for a beauty like you. Who wouldn't like a fur-lined cradle and warm water to wash in? I would my-self. So would everyone else. But crying won't help; oh no, not at all. Keeps you awake, and your poor mother. It's all finished now. Now you'll stop. Look, I'm going to put you down like this, that's right, on top of the shawl, and I'm going to wrap you tight, tight and snug . . . like you've never been wrapped before . . . there . . . a very neat bundle. Lovely. And now there's no more nonsense. You're going to sleep."

"How can you wrap her like that?" Golda burst out. "It's too tight. You'll squeeze her to death . . . please."

"Nonsense. It makes them feel safe if they're tightly wrapped. See, she's stopping . . . her eyelids are droop-ing. She'll be asleep soon."

Rachel and Golda stared. Rachel said, "How did you do that? It's magic!"

Clara laughed. "It's not magic, I promise you. It's because I'm not nervous. Babies, they're like animals. They smell fear and worry and tiredness. They smell it in the person who's holding them. You can't pretend. They hear it in your voice . . . everything." She turned to Golda. "There, let's put her down. She'll sleep now, but not for long."

"Why not?" Golda asked. "Why not for long? I thought that after the whole night . . ."

"Golda, I must talk to you like a mother. Do you understand? I'm not your mother. I'm almost a stranger, but I must talk as if I were your closest relation.

Haven't you asked yourself why she was crying all night?"

"Haven't I asked? What else have I been doing but asking and asking, again and again."

"I'll tell you," Clara said. "She's hungry. There's nothing wrong with her. She's just terribly, terribly hungry."

"But how can she be? I feed her myself. She's the only person here who's being regularly fed with the best food there is . . . milk from her mother."

"The milk from her mother is not enough."

Golda was shouting now. "Not enough? How can it be not enough? It's all I've got. I haven't got anything else. It has to be enough. If you have a baby, you have milk in your breasts to feed that baby. It's natural. Dogs, cows, goats, cats—they have enough. Why not me? I've always had enough. What's the matter with me? Why should I be different?"

"Golda, relax, calm down," Clara said firmly. "Sit. It happens sometimes that there is not enough milk, that's all. It isn't anybody's fault. It happens. Maybe the mother is sick—"

"I'm *not* sick!" Golda's eyes blazed.

"But you haven't eaten or drunk properly for some time. You're tired and you're worried and you're losing your milk."

"So she'll die. That's all. That's what you're telling me. She'll die, because I have no milk and there's not another drop of liquid on this stinking ship that's going to pass her lips and give her cholera or typhoid or—God, what will I do? What am I going to do?" Golda flung herself down on the bunk, sobbing.

Clara spoke firmly now. "I'll tell you what you're going to do. You're going to stop crying and pull yourself together. You're not the first woman whose milk has gone, and you won't be the last. Stop feeling sorry for yourself and think of the baby. If she doesn't drink milk, she'll starve to death. Therefore the solution is simple. We will find milk."

Golda had stopped sobbing, but said nothing.

Rachel whispered, "Where will we find it?"

"Somewhere on this ship there is milk," said Clara. "We will take it even if the Captain has to drink black coffee all the way to America. And meanwhile, Golda, sleep. Rest. Rachel and I will look after the baby. Drink water, suckle your child. Your milk may come back. Who knows?"

I am nothing, Golda thought as sleep engulfed her. Nothing. Not even as important as a cow. I have no milk for my child.

Clara was sitting beside Mr. Kaminsky holding the

baby. "I have sent Mina to ask about milk." She sighed. "We all need food. You don't cry all night like this little thing, but you, too, I haven't seen eating at all."

Mr. Kaminsky said, "I'll tell you the truth, Mrs. Zussmann, I'm not hungry. It's of very little importance to me now, food. That's even when I'm not on a ship. But here? Who can eat? Who wants to?"

"You have to eat, Mr. Kaminsky," Clara said, "or you will become weak and ill, and what will your relatives in America think?"

"Listen, Mrs. Zussmann. You are a good woman. You are kind to me. I am grateful. I am also not too old to see that you are a fine woman, a handsome woman, a person. A proper person. As I said, I am grateful. But I will tell you something I have told no one, ever before. God knows it, because he can look into my heart and see it, but so far he has taken no notice of my wishes. I think he is punishing me."

"Punishing you?" said Clara. "Why should he punish you? What have you done? A good, kind man like you?"

"He is punishing me because I want . . . not to live any more."

"Not live?" Clara was astonished. "Why do you say such a terrible thing? Who can not want to live?"

The old man hardly heard her. "They died," he said. "So many of them. Or were hurt. I hid in my poor wife's linen basket. Even from there I could hear the shrieking, like a million devils from hell. Every moment,

I thought someone would find me. I thought they would burn the house. It seemed to go on for many hours. It seemed to me that I was dead already and that this was to be my life after death. But in the end, there was silence, and I crawled out, and I wish that I had not crawled out. I wish I had stayed in that basket and suffocated to death. There were people in the streets . . . dead . . . torn apart . . . terrible . . . and wounds all over them, and all the buildings crackling and burning, a horrible smoke, clouds of black smoke hanging in the sky . . . and moaning. . . . I was looking for my wife, searching among . . . Oh, God, help me, pieces of broken people. I never found her. If I had found her, I would have gone mad. She was in her sister's house. Burned down. Family friends, business friends, enemies, all kinds of people. But not me. I was alive. God must have selected me to suffer, not even allowing me the relief of losing my reason."

Clara sat silent for a while. Looking down, she noticed that she was holding Mr. Kaminsky's hand. His face was wet with tears.

She said, "The world is full of terrible things. But why do you think God is punishing you? Perhaps he has plans to make you happy in America. Perhaps he saved your life just for that."

Mr. Kaminsky chuckled. "At my age? In a new country? What will I do? Who will I be? How will I learn such a language? In Kishinev, I was somebody. There, in America, I will be nobody. An old man with terrible memories, that's all. A burden to my nieces and nephews, because I have no children of my own." He patted his bundles. "Only my books."

"Do they make you happy?" Clara asked.

"Reading them, I can forget the real world. Philosophy, thank God, has very little to do with things as they are."

"Then at least have a sugared almond to give you a sweet taste in your mouth while you read."

Mr. Kaminsky smiled. "You are tempting me, like Eve tempted Adam, and like Adam, I will yield. But only one, thank you."

"Perhaps you would care to accompany me up to the deck? The child is sleeping now. I will leave her with Rachel."

"I have not been up there since we left Hamburg."

"Really? Then come at once. You will feel much better. Much, much better, and maybe even, who knows, hungry?"

"Very well," said Mr. Kaminsky. "I will come and pay a little attention to the sea."

Leaning over the railings, Mr. Kaminsky said nothing for a moment, then, "In Hamburg, in that shed, there was a girl . . . very young . . . I helped her a little. I haven't seen her. Perhaps she is in another part of the ship. She was pregnant. She was very near her time. Perhaps . . ."

Clara's eyes lit up. "You're thinking maybe she's

had the baby . . . maybe she'll have milk, for two babies."

"Maybe she will. If she's had the child . . ."

"I'll find out. Or maybe Mina will have found out something."

Clara

*The air is so sharp, it stings your nostrils, and the wind
is blowing and making white crests on all the waves.
But the sky is clear, like a glass dome over us, the kind
of round glass dome confectioners cover cakes with.
I'm so glad he is here, poor man. Let him look at the
sky, how lovely it is, pink and mauve and orange,
like shot silk, all the colors blurring into one another
and fading, up there, into a color that's not blue or
gray or pink . . . who can call it a name? Like
mother-of-pearl, glowing. The sun has gone now,
and all the water from here to the horizon is pink,
red almost, and shining. Mr. Kaminsky is staring at the
water, not speaking. Perhaps all the red reminds him
of blood. How stupid! I'm not thinking. I'm thinking
of the baby. I'm an old fool. No one but a fool would
have brought him here at sunset. Perhaps I should
suggest we go and look over the other side. The water
is not so red there. The night will soon be here.*

Chapter 5

"WHERE DO WE BEGIN?" ASKED MINA. "WHO SHOULD WE ask. We must ask someone."

"The Captain?" Daniel suggested.

"They'd never let us get up there. And anyway, I don't think captains deal with things like milk for babies. What about one of those stewards, the ones who give the food out each day?"

"That's right. They'd know. We'd better try to find them somewhere . . ."

"Where?"

"In the galley. That's what you call a kitchen on a ship."

"I know that," Mina snapped. "Come along. We must hurry."

They ran along narrow, ill-lit corridors lined with sheets of painted metal. They peered into small cabins that were always empty. The sound of their feet echoed on the floors. The ship was rolling steadily, so that they slid against the walls as they ran.

"Hey! What's all this then?" A booming voice rang out behind them. Speaking German. "What're you two kids doing down here? It's not allowed. No passengers allowed down here, you know. Go on, back to your compartment. At the double."

Mina and Daniel turned. A big man with tufts of yellowish hair sticking out all over his head and a thick yellow moustache was standing in the passage. His nose was red, and his heavy arms and shoulders were pink and patterned all over with drawings of blue sea serpents and blue mermaids. Mina couldn't stop looking at them.

"Cat got your tongue?" the man asked. "Never seen a tattoo before, eh?"

"What's that?" said Daniel.

"These pictures. They prick the ink in with a needle. It hurts, but it's worth it. They don't ever come off."

"Not even in the water?" Mina was amazed.

"No, not never. Now, I've been patient with you, but enough's enough. Back you go to where you belong."

"Oh, no," cried Mina. "No, we can't. That is, we will, of course, but I mean we need milk. We came down here to look for milk."

"It's not a bloody luxury liner you're on, you know," said the man. "Milk, indeed! Maybe you'd like some iced cakes too, eh?" He laughed, and rubbed his moustache.

"No, you don't understand," said Daniel. "The milk is not for us. It's for a tiny baby."

"Hasn't this baby got a mother, then?" asked the sailor.

"Yes," said Daniel, "but . . ." He blushed.

Mina glared at him. "What he means is, the mother hasn't any milk. The milk has stopped coming. If," she added, "we can't get milk now, from somewhere, any-where, then the baby will die. Do you understand now why we're here?"

"Oh. Aye. Yes. Yes, indeed." The man looked con-fused. "Well, now. Milk. A mother's milk, that will be what the poor mite needs. And . . . wait a minute . . . there's a new mother in the forward compartment. She had her baby about two days ago . . . Maybe—" He paused. "I'll take you to see her. See what she says. She can't speak German. God knows where she comes from. She's not Jewish, though."

"That doesn't matter," said Mina. "Let's go and find her. Please."

As they made their way to the forward compart-ment, Mina asked, "How do you know she's not Jewish?"

"Well, she can't understand German. If she knew Yiddish, she could speak to me, same as you lot can.

It's near enough."

Mina and Daniel peered into the compartment, so much like their own, and yet different, unfamiliar. The bundles on the bunks, the faces of the people . . . Mina hadn't realized how accustomed she had become, and how quickly, to those who lived with her in her new surroundings. The sailor led them through a crush of bodies to a bunk at the far side.

"This is where she is," he said. "In there. Behind that curtain. Can you find your own way back? I've got work to do, and I don't fancy the smell in here, I must admit. Sometimes I wish I worked in the engine room."

"Yes," said Mina. "Thank you. We'll manage. Thank you for helping us."

The sailor smiled at her. "Good luck, then," he said, and pushed his way through the crowd that had formed around Mina and Daniel and stood staring at them with curious eyes.

Mina looked at the nearest person and said, "Does anyone here speak Yiddish or Russian?"

"I do," said an elderly, balding man. "I speak Russian."

"Thank God." Mina sighed. "We come from the aft compartment. There's a baby there. The mother has no milk. Can we speak to the lady who has just had a baby? Can we ask her if she'll feed another child as well as her own?"

"Ask her," said one woman. "Try. She hasn't said one word the whole voyage. Even in labor. Not one word."

"What language shall I speak?" asked Mina.

"Russian," Daniel said. "Try Russian. And I know a few words of Polish."

"What if she's Hungarian? Or Rumanian? Or Italian?"

"Just ask."

Mina pulled the curtain aside and looked into the bunk. A young woman lay there, a baby wrapped in a dirty shawl beside her. Vacant eyes stared at Mina without seeing her.

"Hello," Mina whispered. "What a lovely baby. What is it? Is it a girl or a boy?"

The woman said nothing.

"Listen." Mina knelt beside her. "I must ask you something. A baby is dying where we are. The mother has no milk. Please can we bring the child to you? Will you feed her? Please, I beg of you. This baby will die if she doesn't have milk. Will you? Please nod or make some sign if it's all right. Do something. Please. It's very important."

The woman gazed at Mina for a long time. Then, almost imperceptibly, she moved her head.

"Did you nod?" cried Mina. "Thank you, oh, thank you." She bent down and kissed the unknown, silent, kindly person who was going to save little Sarah. "I'll go and fetch her at once. Thank you."

The pale lips moved: "What's your name?"

Mina smiled. At last, she thought, she is speaking. I did it. I made her speak.

"Mina Isaacs," she said. "What's yours?"

But the silence had returned. The woman stared fixedly at the wall as though Mina had not existed.

As they left to fetch Golda's baby, Mina thought she heard someone muttering. A woman said, "I wouldn't do it. Not for a Jewish baby. What's one more or less . . ."

She turned to Daniel, who was staring straight ahead and seemed to have heard nothing at all. Perhaps I imagined it, thought Mina. But I know I didn't. She felt her anger rising, longed to go and shake whoever had said such a thing by the hair till her teeth rattled, but that would spoil everything. Golda's baby must have milk. Nothing else was important. Nothing.

The young woman watched Mina leave the compartment, her hair like a torch shining. So red. She knows nothing about me and yet she seems to trust me. She seems even to like me. Me, Olga Vilenska. She wanted to talk to me, but what can I say? That I am feeling now as if I don't exist? That this baby of mine seems like a stranger to me, a person who has nothing to do with me, even though she was so long a part of my body. The girl wouldn't understand. I am not much older than she is, not in years; but in what has happened to me—there, I am old, old, old. Maybe a hundred years old.

Would that girl know what I meant if I told her? My father threw me out of the house because I was pregnant, and my mother and sisters cried all the way down the road after me, running at the last moment and thrusting jewelry into my hands saying, "Sell it. Sell it and go to America. Start another life." The road to the railway station seemed so long. It was still hot then. The end of summer.

Golda was sobbing. "How can I? Oh, God help me, how can I? Not very clean, Mina said, and my Sarah, how can I let you? We don't know this woman. She sounds dreadful. Mad, even. Mina said she hasn't spoken a word the whole voyage. My Sarah . . . she'll get some terrible disease . . ."

Clara slapped her face. "Stop it at once, Golda. You're being hysterical. Now calm down. God has been good and sent a nursing mother on this trip, into this hell-hole, and you dare to worry about dirt, and who she is? What do you care? Your Sarah will have a very terrible disease called death before very long, if you don't take her at once. Now."

"I can't." Golda's sobs had subsided and she sniffed. "I couldn't. I don't want to see that woman. I couldn't bear it."

"You're a silly girl," said Clara softly. "You'll take her in the end. You'll see. Today you're tired. Mina and Rachel and I will take the baby in turn, till you're ready. Every four hours."

"What about the night?" Golda sighed.

"What about it? Night, day, it's all the same. To Sarah, and to me." Clara sighed. "I'll go in the night."

"I've got a chess set," said Daniel. "Shall I teach you?"

"No, I don't feel like it now," Mina said. "Maybe another time."

"What shall we do then?"

"I don't know. I don't really feel like doing anything. We can talk."

"What shall we talk about?"

"You can't decide beforehand," Mina said crossly. "You just talk. It happens all by itself."

"I never know where to start."

"I'll start. Tell me about your grandparents. Why did you run away?"

"I didn't like it there," said Daniel. "I wasn't used to it. Before"—he paused—"before, when my parents were alive, when I was small, I lived on a farm. There was space all around. And trees, and animals."

"What did your parents die of?" Mina asked.

"Of cholera."

"And you went to your grandparents. What was wrong with them?"

"They lived in the town. It was hot and dusty in the summer, and all the houses were squeezed together, and in the winter all the roads were muddy . . ."

"But there must have been mud on the farm as well? . . ." Mina looked hard at him.

"Yes, there was, but it was different." Daniel sighed. "I suppose, the truth is my grandparents were not good people. I don't think they really wanted me to live with them, but they had to . . . I was their daughter's child, after all—" Daniel stopped.

"Go on." Mina leaned forward.

"I've never told anyone this."

"Tell me."

He took a deep breath. "They treated me like a servant. All day long, I was fetching and carrying and cutting logs and drawing water and going to the market to get the food. All that, and going to school. I hardly had any time just for myself. I worked hard, and I didn't mind very much, only there was one place I hated. I hated going there. The cobbler's."

"Why?"

"He was a horrible looking man. He had no teeth, and he spoke in a cracked voice, and one of his eyes was blind. He frightened me. He used to hold my coat in his fingers. I hated his shop. It smelled of dead animals. All the skins lay in a pile, and he cut them up for shoes. One day my grandmother sent me on my own. I was only eight. I had to wait while he mended the shoes and then bring them back. He told me horrible things. I was nearly sick."

"What things?"

"Well, now I realize he was probably a little mad, poor man. But I was young then and I . . . he said if I was naughty, if anyone was naughty . . . he came in the night and stripped their skins off and dried them and made them into shoes for fine ladies."

Mina said nothing.

"After that, I asked, begged, cried to my grandmother to please never, never send me there again. But she did. She said I was being a baby, and it was all nonsense. So when I was old enough, I wrote to my uncle, and he sent me a ticket. There was nothing my grandparents could do. I ran away, and here I am." Daniel smiled. "I've never told anyone before."

"I'm glad you told me. Weren't you scared, running away?"

"No, since I left that town, I've been happy." He laughed. "I don't think I'll ever be as frightened of anything as I was of that old cobbler. It's good to think that the worst thing of all is over already."

"Why don't you want to live with your uncle in New York?"

"No, not in a big town. I'm going to California."

"Won't you be lonely?" Mina asked. "You don't know anyone in California."

"I'll meet new people. I don't mind that. And maybe you will write to me."

"Yes," said Mina. "I'll write to you, if you answer."

"I'll answer." Daniel looked at Mina, then quickly looked away. Mina opened her mouth to speak, but something in the way Daniel was sitting made her change her mind, and she said nothing.

Rachel sat on the bunk behind the makeshift curtain and watched Sarah sucking greedily on the silent woman's breast. At first she had turned her eyes away, not wishing to embarrass this kind person, but her eyes were drawn back to the round blue-veined globe of flesh, full of milk, and to Sarah's moist pink mouth opening and closing like a seaflower. This woman, she's not much older than me, Rachel thought. It could be me, lying there in the bunk, holding a child. She looked down at herself, at the front of her dress, and wondered whether she, too, would swell and fill until her breasts became as round and heavy as melons. Why doesn't she speak? Why does she never look at her baby or smile at it, Rachel wondered. Is her husband waiting for her? Perhaps her husband is dead. There had been girls in the village who had given birth to children with no husband at all, and the older women had clicked their tongues and shaken their heads and frowned at the disgrace. Perhaps this woman was one of those. I wish, Rachel thought, I wish that I was her. I wish that I hadn't been so modest, so virtuous. What good did it do me? It seemed then as if there was all the time in the world, and there wasn't. I could be holding Chaim's baby now. Sarah had finished sucking. She was fast asleep. Rachel picked her up and wrapped a shawl around her.

"Thank you," she said softly. The young woman in the bunk looked briefly at Rachel, but said nothing. She picked up her own child and put it to the breast without even turning her head.

Any child born to this one, thought Olga, will know his father. Grow up with him. She knows the proper order of things in a way that I didn't. But my child could have had a father. Alexander would have married me. All my childhood and youth he lived in the same street, loving me. And I wouldn't even speak to him. So plain. So simple. How could I feel for him as I felt for Mikhail? I didn't know that Mikhail would leave so soon and never come back, even though he said he would. I believed him. When he didn't come, I made up my mind never to believe anyone ever again. Never to trust anyone else. Only myself.

Rachel made her way carefully through the bundles on the floor, and struggled up the companionway on to the deck. An image of Yasha Dubowsky smiling at her flickered in the corners of her mind as she bent her head against the wind, buzzed at the edge of her thoughts like a small insect. She pushed it away impatiently and thought about Chaim. It was becoming more and more difficult to remember exactly what he looked like.

"Daniel showed me his chess set," said Eli. "There are some horses in it, and also kings and queens and castles. The kings and queens don't look like kings and queens, though."

"I know. He showed me too," said Mina. "Listen, Eli, I want to tell you something. When we get to America, there will be people who might ask you questions. I'm going to help you learn what to answer. You must answer straight away and nice and clearly. No dreaming about. Do you understand?"

"Yes. I think so. What questions?"

"What is your name, how old are you, what is your father's name, those sorts of questions."

Eli frowned. "I can answer those. They're not hard. They won't ask me to do sums, will they, or read from the Bible?"

"No, no, I'm sure they won't. Just stand up straight and try to look happy and don't chew your handkerchief, and I'm sure you'll be all right."

"I didn't know we had to answer questions."

"Yes, and a doctor will look at you, too," said Mina. Clara Zussmann had told her about the doctors. "Just to see that you're in good health." Mina remembered lying awake on winter nights listening to her little brother wheezing and coughing. Perhaps his chest was weak. Did they let in people with weak chests? Was a weak chest the same as tuberculosis? Surely one of the reasons for going to America was to make certain that the chests of the children grew stronger, that their health improved? Eli looked thin. They all looked thin because the food was so horrible. Did he look worse than anyone else? Mina doubted it. Only Yankel Katz was just as fat and horrible as he had been at the beginning of the journey. His mother seemed to have an unending supply of tasty bits and pieces, morsels that she hoarded for her son. Nothing was too good for precious Yankele.

"Where's Daniel?" asked Eli.

"Up on the deck, I think."

"Why aren't you with him? You're his friend."

"I don't have to be with him every minute of the day, you know," Mina snapped, and was immediately sorry. "Come, I'll draw a farm. Tell me what animals we should have."

Eli's face lit up: "Chickens and goats and cows and horses and cats and dogs and—"

"Wait a minute! Wait a minute! One at a time." She laughed and began to sketch in a cow with fat, spotted flanks and long horns. She tried not to think about what Daniel was doing. If I get too friendly, she thought, if I grow to like him too much, then it will be terrible never to see him again. She put in the feathers of a chicken with swift strokes of her pencil, and wondered. Surely it was wrong, what she was feeling? Surely at her age she shouldn't be like this, seeing his face in front of her eyes all the time, like those stupid people who mooned about in love? Wasn't she too young? Maybe I will ask Rachel, she thought. If I can find the words.

It happened sometimes, Clara knew. She looked at the silent mother, who had turned towards the wooden partition to sleep and thought: But surely I was never as bad as this? When David was born I had all the love and attention in the world, and David was beautiful and I loved him with all my heart, and everyone came with gifts and flowers, and I lay in the big bed and cried and cried and didn't want to see anyone, and Mama pleaded with me, and Isaac pleaded with me, and I lay there and wished, wished that it had never happened, that I was anywhere but in that bed, pressed under such weights of feeling that I couldn't talk to anyone about anything. It passes, that's true. Now, when I think of it, it's as if it wasn't me, but someone else, another person. Having children does something strange to you. It changes you completely. Do they realize, the younger ones? Does Golda realize that never, not for one instant of her life, will she be without some part of her wondering, asking, worrying, loving her child? Do they know it is forever? And do they understand what a strain, what a burden, what a load such huge and overwhelming love can be? The joy they know about. Everybody speaks of it all the time, but the aches and millions of tiny worries and large worries, the fears that you can never let them see? Do they know about that? I think that a mother's heart must be just like a pincushion. I had one when I was a girl. It even had the shape of a heart. Red velvet. My own mother helped me to make it. All the silver pins I stuck into it shone like tiny drops of rain, but deep inside the cushion, that was where all the sharp points of the pins were hidden. That's what it's like: all the pleasures, all the happiness glitters on the surface, and all the sharp sorrows are buried so that no one can see them.

Clara wrapped little Sarah tightly in her shawl and stood up. Two o'clock in the morning, she thought, was a terrible time to think about anything. In the morning, when she was not so tired, she would be herself, and not so gloomy. Hearts and pincushions, indeed. Just old age and tiredness talking in her head, giving her these thoughts.

Olga thought: this baby, which should be precious to me because she should remind me of Mikhail, reminds me of no such thing. Her birth was soon over, and all through it I said nothing, did not cry out, but as soon as she was born, the tears kept coming. Not tears of pain, but of loneliness. Suddenly, having her, not being alone any more, made me feel worse than ever before, worse than when I left home. I am frightened of being responsible for her, for everything. I am frightened of having brought her into a life that I cannot know about. How will it be for her? For me? For the little Jewish baby, Sarah? For any of us, over there, far away from our homes?

Clara made her way through the compartment quietly, so as not to wake anyone, and pulled the shawl around Sarah's head to protect her from the sea wind.

Daniel

*If I can't be a farmer, I'll be a sailor. Today, the sea
is almost like the land, dark, like a plowed field, with
rows and rows of white wave tops, like small, growing
plants. If you are a sailor, the sky is never too close
to you. There is room to breathe, more room than
on the land, really, and here you are, snug in this little
house, this ship, bobbing up and down right in the
middle of it, safe. No one else seems to like it very
much. They moan about the food, the cold, the smells—
everything. I must be the one that's mad. It can't be
that I'm right and everyone else is wrong. I like it.
I can be with people when I want to be and also
come up here when I want to be without them. I like
to talk to Mina. I like to see her draw. One day, I will
ask her to untie her plaits. If her hair was all spread out,
it would ripple like a stretch of water, like the sea,
only a lovely red and gold, like wheat, or leaves in
autumn or . . . something. It looks soft, like smooth
animal fur, and sometimes I want to reach out and
stroke it, stroke Mina like a cat, but probably she would
hit me and then not talk to me. It's not worth trying.*

Chapter 6

MRS. KATZ DRAGGED YANKEL OVER TO THE WASH BASINS by his ear.

"I'm not listening to one single word," she shrieked. "You tell me you wash, and tonight I saw your neck, and Heaven preserve me from ever seeing such blackness again. Open your collar."

"But, Mother," whined Yankel, "you can't. Not in front of everyone, not like a baby. I'll do it myself, I promise."

"Open your collar!" Mrs. Katz's eyes were blazing. She dipped a rag torn from an old sheet into the water and began scrubbing her son's neck with the zeal of a good housewife polishing neglected brass.

"What's the matter with you? Stand still," she muttered from between clenched teeth. "Aren't you looking forward to the party?"

"It won't be proper," gasped Yankel. "No proper food or anything. No cakes."

"At least you'll be clean. Turn around. Give me your face."

Yankel sighed and closed his eyes. That Mina was staring at him. He knew it even with his eyes closed. She'd be sorry. He thought about Eli's horse. Tonight, at the party, no one would be looking at him. Some people had bottles of brandy. No one would be guarding their luggage. Halfway to America, everyone thought they knew everyone else well enough to trust them a little. Yankel laughed.

"What are you snorting about, young man?" said his mother. "Give me your hands." She waved a pair of scissors in front of him. "Did you think you were going to get away with nails like that?"

Rachel's father thought of Rachel's other birthdays and frowned. There was nothing to give her here, no Panya to fill the house with baking smells and candles, not even a pretty dress to wear. What way was this to become eighteen, to become a woman? Still, everyone was being kind, he noticed that. Mrs. Zussmann had spent the morning pushing bundles and cases to one side, clearing a space in the middle of the floor. "In case the young people want to dance," she said. All around him people were tidying, combing, cleaning, scrabbling in their luggage for bits and pieces of festive clothing. We need a celebration, he thought. We are halfway to America. We are tired of sadness. We need an excuse to forget our troubles and be happy, if only for a little while. I am glad my Rachel's birthday is a reason for happiness. Last night, when I showed her the little ring her mother had asked me to give her on this day, she wept. Perhaps she realizes that she will never see her mother again. I dare not speak of it to her in case she is still hoping. How can I destroy her hope? I remember how she looked in Panya's arms minutes after she was born. She looked at me then just as she does today.

Mina rolled up the paper very carefully and tied it with a ribbon from her hair.

"What are you doing?" said Hannah. "That's your best ribbon."

"It's a present for Rachel. Only a drawing, but I haven't got anything else. It doesn't matter about the ribbon. I've got others."

"Not such good ones." Hannah sniffed. "Let's see

the drawing. I expect you think in America ribbons grow on trees."

Mina laughed. "Wouldn't it be a lovely tree if they did: all bows in satin and velvet and silk and all different colors." She spread the drawing out on the bunk. "It's not as good as I wanted it to be. But I used the very best piece of paper I had."

Hannah looked. It was a picture of Rachel standing on the deck, looking out to sea. A wind was blowing her skirts out behind her, and her hair was flying around her face. On that small piece of paper, the drawing was alive with movement and life, and Rachel's smile shone out, like her real smile.

"It's beautiful," whispered Hannah. "It's really beautiful. You have a talent." She smiled at her daughter. "I'm sorry if I made your life a misery nagging you about the piano all those years. This is what you must do. Perhaps in America—" She stopped.

"Yes?" Mina asked. "What?"

"Perhaps one day there will be enough money for a good teacher. Maybe an art school when you're older . . ."

Mina flung her arms around her mother's neck. "Of course, there will be . . . thank you! In America, there is enough money for everything!"

Hannah smiled. "Go and give Rachel your present, and then come back here. I'll pin your plaits up, just for tonight."

Mina jumped off the bunk and ran to find Rachel.

Golda was quite herself again now that Sarah was being properly fed. She had unearthed a gown of crimson shot silk and had decked herself with every available piece of jewelry, so that she shone from the top of her shiny, dark hair to the buckles on her best shoes. Rachel sat on the trunk in front of her, submissive and quiet.

Golda said, "Now, I don't want one objection, do you hear? It's your birthday. You're eighteen now, and if it kills me, I'm going to make you beautiful so that no one will know you. Wait till you see what I'm doing to your hair."

"I can feel," said Rachel. "And anyway, I'm not sure I want to go unrecognized."

"Ssh!" Golda wielded the comb and brush. "Hold these pins. Now. This bit up here, and twist that . . . so. Give me a pin . . . two . . . there." She looked happily at the back of Rachel's head. "Oh, my goodness, he'll die! Yasha will die of pleasure. Look." She took out a tiny mirror and gave it to Rachel. "Can you see? I'm sorry it's so small. What kind of idiots made this ship anyway, without decent mirrors?"

"I can't see very well," said Rachel, "but I trust you."

"It's beautiful," Golda assured her. "All curls and twists and golden loops here at the back. I never knew I had such a gift. Now," she whispered, "the final touches. Here," (she came and knelt in front of Rachel) "give me your mouth."

"Are you painting my mouth?" Rachel drew back in horror. "Never, oh, never!"

"Don't be a silly goose. Just a tiny bit. Come on."

Rachel closed her eyes and sighed.

Golda dabbed a spot of rouge onto her cheek. Rachel's eyes flew open.

"Not rouge! Oh, Golda, honestly. I'll look . . . I don't know how I'll look."

"You look like a person should look on her eighteenth birthday. See." She held out the mirror. "Not like a plucked chicken any more." She laughed. "Just wait till he sees you!" She hugged herself and rocked from foot to foot.

"Golda! If you don't stop hinting and winking and saying things about Yasha Dubowsky, I'll take off all this rouge and pull out all the pins and your fine work will be undone." Rachel's eyes blazed.

"Temper! Temper!" Golda replied. "Why would you get so cross if he meant nothing to you? I know all the signs, believe me."

"What signs?"

"I've seen you two, walking on the deck."

"We talk, that's all. He's very cheerful. It's pleasant to talk to him."

"He thinks," said Golda, "that it's more than pleasant to talk to you."

"Why? Has he said anything?" Rachel tried to keep her voice as even as possible.

"This and that, this and that. I can tell these things. Besides, he's been running all over the ship trying to find a present for you. That I do know."

"How did he know it was my birthday? I only told Clara yesterday. She only started arranging it this morning."

"You told me a long time ago. Remember? It was when we were still in Hamburg." Golda smiled.

"And you . . ." Words failed Rachel. She picked up the hairbrush and flung it across the floor. "You're an interfering busybody! That's what you are. I'm sorry I let you persuade me into all this."

Golda said, "I'm sorry, Rachel. Don't be angry, please. Not on your birthday. Here, I've got a present for you, too. Just a last finishing touch."

Rachel blushed. "I'm sorry, Golda. I'm sorry I was angry. But you shouldn't, really . . . and I don't need presents, honestly."

"Nonsense, it'll look lovely. Here." She draped a lacy shawl around Rachel's shoulders.

"You can't give me this. It's your best lace shawl." Rachel was aghast.

"I can and I will; and anyway, it's only my second-best. Besides"—she laughed, dabbing a little eau de cologne behind her ears—"in America, I shall have a different shawl for every day of the week, so there."

Rachel stood up, feeling like a different person.

What has Yasha found to give me, she thought, and then quickly tried to think about something else. What has he said to Golda, she wondered. I can never ask, because that would give her ideas and she'd never stop teasing me. Probably she made it all up. She is capable of anything.

"It's amazing," Clara said. "Really amazing. If I'd known, we would have organized a festivity every night. Just look what we've got: dried fruit and some biscuits and brandy. Even a bottle of wine, and someone with an accordion, and people bringing out their finery. Even you"—she smiled at Mr. Kaminsky—"putting on a clean collar, and maybe even a smile. It's done you good, just helping me to clear the floor."

"There is a time to weep and a time to dance," said Mr. Kaminsky. "This, you have decreed, is a time to dance, and I'm not brave enough to fight a woman like you."

"I shall expect you to do more than that," said Clara firmly. "I shall expect you to dance with me."

"For that I escaped the pogrom?" Mr. Kaminsky laughed. "You are a cruel and demanding woman."

"It'll do you good," said Clara firmly. "You'll feel a different man."

"Everybody looks strange," said Eli. "I saw Yankel Katz being washed. He screamed and yelled."

Daniel laughed. "He doesn't look much better, though. Not really."

"Will there be a cake?" asked Eli.

"No, I don't think so." Daniel spoke absentmindedly. He had just caught sight of Mina with her hair up. She looked much older, unfamiliar, a secret person he didn't know.

"I think Mina looks funny," said Eli.

"Yes." Daniel nodded.

"But quite nice."

"Yes. Quite nice." Under the grown-up hair, the face was still the same after all.

Yasha looked down at the floor.

"Could I speak with you, please?" he whispered.

"Yes, of course," said Rachel. "What is it?"

"Not here. Could we go up on the deck, do you think?"

"If you like . . . but . . ."

"Please . . ." Yasha looked at her.

"Very well." Rachel drew the lace shawl up over her head to protect her hair from the wind and followed Yasha up to the deck. They stood beside the railing.

"I have a present for your birthday," he said, turning to face her.

She blushed. "That's very kind of you. You didn't have to give me a present."

"I wanted to give you . . . something marvelous." Yasha grinned at her. "Jewels. Something precious. Something . . . worthy of you." He thrust a package into her hands. "But, well, there it is. I hope your birthday is a very happy one."

"Thank you." She opened the small parcel. "Oh! It's beautiful. Where did you find it? It's lovely. A lovely box, and look how these flowers and trees and small birds are carved on to the lid. It's . . . I think it's a wonderful present. You couldn't have found anything better."

"One day, I'll—" Yasha said, and stopped.

"Yes?"

"Nothing. I'm glad you liked it." He smiled. He had been about to tell her, about to say: one day, I shall fill it to the top with jewels for you . . . but he couldn't.

He didn't know what she would think. Perhaps such words would frighten her away. When I speak to her, he thought, I feel as though she's a bird, a butterfly, something fragile that the least hasty movement will frighten away. I feel so huge and clumsy, as if I might hurt her.

"Thank you very much, Yasha," Rachel said. "I really do thank you."

"Rachel, will you dance with me tonight?" he whispered.

"I don't know." She looked down at the deck. "Everyone will be watching. I'm not good at dancing."

"I'll show you. I'll help you. Please. Just one dance on your birthday."

"Very well." She smiled at him. "Come, we'll go down where it's warmer."

Just before they went into the crowded compartment, Yasha pulled her back.

"I forgot to tell you up there . . ."

"What?" She could feel the warmth of his hand on her arm.

I love you, he wanted to say. I love you and I want to hold you and be with you, and I've never felt any of these things before, and they make me feel . . . I don't know how they make me feel. He said, "I think you look very pretty tonight."

"Thank you," said Rachel. "And for the lovely present."

"You won't forget our dance? You promised."

"I won't forget."

She walked to her bunk. He will hold me around the waist, she thought, tightly around the waist, and the thought of being so close to him made her feel suddenly weak. She sat down quickly on the bunk and traced with her finger the carvings on the lid of the wooden box.

It was late. The party had been a success, Clara thought. Golda had danced with everyone, even taught Mr. Kaminsky how to waltz. Yankel Katz had eaten as much of everything as he could. Mina and Daniel had sat together watching the dancing, listening to the music. The songs that had been sung . . . oh, the old songs, the songs that would always be sung, songs of home. Hannah Isaacs had cried a little, drunk a little brandy. Everyone had had a little brandy. And Rachel, Rachel, the birthday child, how lovely she looked! For once her cheeks were pink, from rouge or brandy or what? Clara smiled. All evening people had crowded around her. That poor young Dubowsky had watched from the other side of the room, unable to get near her. Perhaps now, now that the old people are falling asleep, and the children, too, now that the food is finished and all the brandy nearly gone, perhaps now they will dance together. Soon it will be time to take Sarah for her feed. Soon it will be midnight.

I am so tired, Mr. Kaminsky thought as he lay down. What possessed me tonight, dancing like a youth when all I am is a bundle of old bones held together God knows how. Or why. He chuckled, thinking of Golda's flushed cheeks. Her bright eyes. Youth is like a disease, he thought. Sometimes it is almost infectious. It infected me a little tonight. The drinking of brandy, too, affects the brain, deludes a person into thinking he is something other than what he really is. But it is midnight now and like Cinderella, my glory is fading away. Nothing but rags and tatters left. I feel as though I never want to wake up ever again.

"May I have the pleasure of this dance?" Yasha said. Rachel looked up.

"Yes. I thought you had forgotten."

"Never." Yasha smiled. "How could I forget? I've just given the man playing the accordion another drink and told him to play his sweetest music just for us. This is the first time I've seen you sitting on your own."

He slipped an arm around her waist, and they began to dance. The music was slow at first, waltz-time, and Rachel leaned away from Yasha, feeling shy of all the watching people.

"Close your eyes," whispered Yasha. "Listen to the music. I won't let you fall. I'll hold you."

"Yes," Rachel whispered and closed her eyes. The music grew faster. Yasha's arm around her waist tightened its hold. Round and round she went, and the brandy and the warmth of his body near hers, the heat of the room, made the music grow in her head like a beautiful flower, until she forgot the people watching and was conscious only of her body, turning and turning, and the strong arm behind her, holding her, and the warm breath on her brow, on her hair, and the hard, strange feeling of another body next to hers, so close, touching. She opened her eyes in horror, and pulled away. Yasha was smiling at her.

"That's right," he said. "That's how you should dance. That's lovely."

"Can we stop now?" Rachel whispered. "Please. I want to stop. I need some air. It's so hot."

"Come up on the deck. Look, everyone is nearly asleep. Come."

He is still holding me around the waist, thought
Rachel, and we finished dancing minutes ago.

Yankel was so excited he couldn't sleep. He had
done it at last. Under all their fuddled noses, while they
were busy singing and laughing and dancing, while
Mina and Daniel were sitting close together on the other
side of the compartment, while his mother was busy
talking to some old woman or other. It hadn't taken
more than a minute. He had slipped his hand into the
bundle and felt about until he found something hard,
and then he'd hidden it under his jacket and pushed it
right into his own private bundle, the one his mother
hardly ever looked at. Tomorrow, that snot-nosed little
Eli would find it was missing and what a fuss and to-do
that would cause. They would never find it, of course,
but perhaps it would be safer simply to throw it overboard, then no one could have any proof that it was he
who had taken it. Getting it up to the deck was going
to be a problem, though. There were always people
about. I'll think about it tomorrow, Yankel decided, and
then closed his eyes and yawned and drifted into sleep.

"Did you see them, Daniel?" Mina said. "They've gone up on deck. At this hour. They went ages ago, and they haven't come back."

"Who?" Daniel asked.

"Rachel and Yasha. Did you see them dancing? Didn't Rachel look lovely? I wish I could look like that."

"You look perfectly all right as you are."

Mina said nothing. I mean, she thought, that I wish I could *be* like that, dance like that. I wish Daniel would look at me the way Yasha looked at Rachel. I saw him. A shiver ran up and down her back.

"I expect they're in love," she said. "Don't you think so?"

"I don't know. I think all that love, and things like that, are . . . silly. Why can't people just be friends?"

"I suppose you're right. It doesn't seem to make people very happy."

"No. They cry a lot and swoon and behave like idiots. They never talk properly. It's all just kissing and cuddling."

"Have you ever kissed anyone?" Mina was curious.

"No. Have you?"

"No. But maybe we should, just to see what it feels like."

"All right," said Daniel. "I don't see what everyone makes such a fuss about. You just put your lips like this on someone else's. What's so special about lips?" He leaned forward swiftly and kissed Mina on the mouth. "There. Are you going to faint or swoon?"

"No. But it felt quite nice," said Mina. "Didn't you think so?"

"It was all right, I suppose," said Daniel quietly.

They sat in silence for a while, then Mina said, "I'm going to sleep now. Goodnight."

"Goodnight, Mina. I'm going, too."

As she undid her plaits, Mina hoped that Daniel had not guessed how she felt about his kiss. She fell asleep thinking of that moment, wishing she could make it happen all over again.

She went outside with him, thought Abraham, up there on that freezing deck with nothing over that thin dress but her shawl. And when she danced with him, that was the first time since Chaim died that she has really looked happy. She looked like she used to when she was a girl. She looked like Panya. I shouldn't begrudge her her pleasure. But him: What is he? Where is he from? Who is his family? I know nothing. Is it right to entrust my Rachel to his care? Will he be . . . understanding? He seems a hot-blooded young man . . . perhaps he will take liberties, offend her, hurt her again. She, who has already been hurt so badly. Perhaps I should go up there and see . . . but if there is nothing to see? Maybe they are simply talking. I should not be hasty. No. But perhaps tomorrow I will speak to Rachel about the young man in America. I will not force her. I would never force her, but she is a sensible girl; she will see the advantages for everyone. When we arrive in America, she will forget this Yasha Dubowsky.

Abraham turned over in his bunk. A face from long ago, from the time before he met Panya, came into his mind. What had her name been? His own father had quickly seen to it that they did not meet too often, and then, of course, the family had left the village altogether and he never saw her again. But he hadn't forgotten her. Not at all. The truth is, he thought, that you never do forget, not entirely. It doesn't matter what follows. If I could rush up there and snatch Rachel back from the edge of that abyss they call love, then I would. But I saw her eyes tonight and I fear it is too late. Still, I will talk to her tomorrow.

Rachel

*All the stars are out tonight. The sea is black, and the
stars are there, too, in the water, making it shine.
There is almost no wind. It is cold. I know it is but I
don't feel it. Perhaps I should not have drunk that wine.
It makes you warm, but it makes you stupid, too.
Even Yasha. He isn't saying a word. He must be cold.
He had to take his arm away from my waist to take
his jacket off. He put it over my shoulders. Perhaps I
should go and sleep. I have never felt less like sleeping
in my life. I want to stay here all night and watch
the stars and listen to the silence. I am eighteen now.
Grown up. The stars are far away, I know, but tonight
they are shining so brightly that I feel I could pick
one out of the sky if I stretched my hand out.*

Chapter 7

"YOU'RE VERY QUIET, RACHEL."

"I'm always quiet," she answered. "It's you who have such a lot to say usually."

"You mean I talk too much. I suppose I do. But now, it seems, I can't find any words."

"I should go," said Rachel. "It's late, and cold, and you standing there without a jacket . . . it's not right. You'll get pneumonia."

"Never!" He laughed. "Look at me."

Rachel looked. Under his shirt the muscles of his shoulders, of his arms, stood out clearly.

"Very well then," she said. "You are as strong as an ox, but strength will not prevent you from catching a chill. We should go inside."

"But everyone is there. I like it here with you. Alone with you."

"Just another minute, then." Rachel smiled. Silence fell between them.

Then: "Some of your hair has come loose," Yasha whispered. "Let me pin it up. Turn around."

Obediently, Rachel turned her back to him. "Golda took such trouble," she said. "But it's late now. It doesn't matter. It will have to be brushed out soon."

"Please let me," said Yasha, and he took a fine strand of hair in his fingers. Almost silver it looked in the starlight. He stroked it gently and twisted it till it seemed to be growing like the tendrils of a plant around his fingers. His hand shook as he bent to secure the curl. A faint smell of powder and warm flesh reached him, and he put both hands on Rachel's shoulders to steady himself, because suddenly he felt light, felt as if his whole body could be blown over the side of the ship and out to sea with one breath. He wanted to speak and could not. Instead, he closed his eyes, and put his lips on Rachel's neck, just where the hair ended and the soft skin began, and drank in the taste of her and the fragrance, which was sweeter than he had imagined possible. He could feel her shoulders, quivering under his hands, but she stood there and did not draw away from him. He moved his mouth from her neck to her hair, and his hands plucked out the pin he had just fastened, and all the other pins, too, so that her hair covered his face like water and ran over his mouth and eyes like moonlight. Still she said nothing. Gently, he turned her to face him. She was looking down.

"Rachel," he whispered. "Rachel." There was no other word in his head, only her name. He wanted to shout it so that the sound carried over the sea and penetrated to the black depths of the ocean. Uncertain, fumbling, he felt for her waist under the thick folds of his own jacket. How warm she was! How small! He felt her moving away.

"Rachel, please. Don't be angry. I couldn't help it . . . you're so lovely."

She looked at him. "Yasha, Yasha, I'm not angry. Don't think that . . . only now I must go."

"Why, Rachel . . . I beg of you . . ."

She took off his jacket and held it out to him. "Please put it on. It's very cold."

Yasha put the jacket on.

"And you? What about you? You're shivering."

"I'm going now. It'll be warm down there."

He reached out and took her hand. "Will you still talk to me tomorrow?" he asked.

"Of course."

"And you're not angry with me?"

"No." She smiled. "Even though you took down my hair that Golda spent such a long time on."

"Goodnight, then," Yasha said softly.

Rachel waved to him as she ran along the deck.

Eli was dreaming. He was on a train just like the train that had taken them across the border and all the way to Hamburg. The train was full. Children were crying. Old people were snoring. Then suddenly, there was no one on the train but himself. Everyone had disappeared, even Mina. He searched for her everywhere, and when he found her, her arms were covered with blue pictures of mermaids and sea serpents and shells, and her hair was blue, too, as if she lived under the water. Eli woke up and lay trembling in the bunk, hardly daring to look over to Mina's end. What if the dream had come true? At last, he peeped over the edge of the blanket and sighed with relief. Just the same as always, with one arm flung out across the pillow. There were no pictures on the skin. Daniel and Mina had told him about the sailor, about the mermaids that could never be washed off, and even though they had explained that it was done with a needle pricking ink into your skin, Eli did not fully believe this and felt that perhaps these pictures might grow on the skin all by themselves, if you weren't careful.

It must be very late, he thought. Everyone is asleep, and all the lights are out. In spite of having Mina there, in the same bunk, and his mother below and all the people squashed into their wooden ledges, Eli felt as though he were completely alone, as though the empty train in his dream were still around him. I will get the horse out, he thought. I know just where he is. I can do it without disturbing anyone. He slipped carefully from under the blanket and jumped down to the floor. All the cases were there, pushed up next to the wall at his mother's feet. He felt with his hands until he came to the right bundle, opened it, and slid his hand inside. His fingers felt soft clothes and nothing else. Perhaps I made a mistake, he thought. Maybe it's in one of the other bags. Maybe even in the suitcase. But I didn't put it back in there, I know. Eli began to look in every bundle. He knew that sometimes he forgot things, forgot where he put them. He even forgot where he was from time to time, so perhaps the horse was in the suitcase after all. He clicked open the catches and waited for a moment, holding his breath to make sure no one had awakened. The noise of the little metal clasps jumping open sounded as loud as pistol shots. No one stirred, and Eli began to search through the suitcase. There were some hard things there: a seven-branched candelabra, a Bible, some boxes, but no horse.

Eli returned to his bunk and lay looking into the darkness. The horse was gone. There was no doubt about it at all. It must be my fault, he thought. I must have put it down somewhere and forgotten where. Maybe it's broken by now. Tears filled Eli's eyes, and he blinked them back. I can't cry, because I'm not a baby anymore. Only babies cry. He thought and thought, and the memory of himself pushing the horse into its usual place just before the music started was clear in his head. Very clear. But sometimes, he told himself, I make mistakes. Maybe that was yesterday. He lay for a long time on his back, thinking and thinking, and the tears fell from his eyes and there was nothing he could do to stop them.

Clara saw Yasha leaning over the side of the ship, staring into the water. What was he doing there at three o'clock in the morning? She herself had just brought Sarah back after her feed and found she could not sleep.

"Mr. Dubowsky?" she said. He jumped back from the railing. "I'm sorry. I startled you. Are you all right? I hope you're not considering jumping in, on a beautiful night like tonight."

Yasha laughed. "It is a beautiful night, isn't it?"

"And you," said Clara, "enjoyed the party. I saw."

Yasha nodded. Clara said, "Do you feel like talking or do you want this chattering old woman to keep her mouth firmly closed and go away and leave you alone?"

"No, no, of course not, Mrs. Zussmann. I want to talk. I want to talk and talk. In fact, to tell you the truth, I want to shout."

Clara nodded and said softly, "It's Rachel, isn't it?"

"Yes," Yasha said. "I don't seem to be able to stop thinking about her. It's like a tune that gets into your head, and you carry it around with you all the time, tangled up with your other thoughts. I try to think about other things: my future, my parents, and all I see is . . . her face."

Clara laughed. "It's called love, Mr. Dubowsky. Love."

"Love?" Yasha looked down into the water. He hadn't given the feeling a name before. To give it a name made it . . . a little frightening.

"What do you think I should do?" he asked.

Clara put a hand on his arm. "It's not for me to tell you what to do. You will know what's right. I'll only say this: be gentle. Don't frighten her away."

Yasha turned and muttered under his breath: "I may have done that already."

"What did you say?"

"Nothing, Mrs. Zussmann. I only hope I know what to do."

"Of course you will. Of course. Now I must go to sleep. If I were forty years younger, I would prefer to stay here with you, but at my age, alas, I must choose peace and quiet."

"Goodnight, Mrs. Zussmann. Thank you."

"Goodnight. And don't worry. Everything will be for the best."

Yasha watched her walking along the deck until

she turned to go below. Then he took the picture of the girl on the swing out of his jacket pocket. Without even glancing at it, he tore it across and across again, several times, until his hand was full of small scraps of cardboard. Smiling, he let them drop out of his hand and fall into the black water below. They bobbed on the surface like tiny fallen stars, and he watched them as they were carried further and further from the ship, until at last they disappeared into the darkness.

"Eli," Mina whispered. "What's the matter?"

"Is it the morning yet?" Eli replied, his voice thick with tears.

"No. It's very early." Mina sat up. "You're crying. Why are you crying? Did you have a bad dream?"

"No. Yes. I did, but that's not—" Eli sat up, too. "Mina, it's the horse. I can't find it. Not anywhere. I've looked in every bundle."

"When? When did you look?"

"In the night. When you were asleep. He's gone."

Mina took a deep breath. "Eli, no one can look for things properly in the night. In the dark. You could easily have missed it. When the real morning comes, then we'll look properly. Try and sleep a little more now. I'll help you look. In the morning."

"He's gone. I know he has."

"Then we'll find him. Where could he have gone? We'll turn the whole compartment inside out, and we'll find him, don't worry."

Eli lay down and closed his eyes. Mina would find the horse. Mina could find anything. Mina could do anything. She would look after him.

Mina looked at Eli. He was sleeping. She pushed the hair away from his eyes. His forehead felt hot. Dry. And his cheeks were flushed. Maybe it was all that crying. Could he be ill? Her whole body turned ice cold. There were only a few more days until they reached America. Would he be better by then? Would they let him in if he were sick? She buried her head in her knees. Oh, please God, she thought, don't let him be sick. Please make it nothing. Make him better quickly. A tiny, horrible worm of a thought wriggled in the back of her mind: Eli might die. She thrust it away from her with a shudder. It's nothing, she told herself. He's been crying all night, that's all it is. Please, please, let the morning come. Let me find his horse. If I can find his horse, he will be better. When will it start being light?

Golda looked at Sarah and smiled. There she is, she thought, full of good milk, her stomach round with it, fast asleep, and here am I, wide awake and thinking of food. I suppose everyone thinks of it, almost all the time, but it's shaming to dream about it too: all the time dreams of stuffed cabbages and thick borscht with globs of sour cream floating on top and little cakes with poppy seeds and honey in them and crusty bread and yellow butter. . . . With a great effort, Golda tore her thoughts away from food and tried to concentrate on something else.

In a few days she would see her husband again. It had been so long, nearly a whole year. Suddenly, Golda felt nervous. After all, they hadn't known one another for very long. A month before the wedding, and two or three months after that. She found that his face was difficult to recall. So many faces here in front of her eyes all the time made it hard to remember. Sometimes, a clear vision of him flashed across her mind, and she tried to keep it with her, reach after it and find it again, but it had gone. Still, she loved him. Of that, she was sure. Hadn't their first meeting been romantic? It was Romeo and Juliet all over again. The families had arranged it, and Golda, for her part, had been overjoyed. She had spent the whole day making herself as clean and pretty as she could. She had spent days before helping her mother to clean the house and bake little biscuits that melted in the mouth. She had never seen Moishe before. He was apprenticed to a tailor in Vilna, but she had heard, through little bits of talk that fell from the lips of her mother's friends, that partly he had been sent far away because of an unsuitable love affair. She had also heard (where? she couldn't remember where) that in Vilna there was someone very beautiful, but also unsuitable, whom he wanted to marry. She, Golda, had been chosen by both families as being the right bride to bring Moishe back to his senses, to stop him from throwing his life away. That was a phrase his mother used constantly. To Golda she had said, "You, my dear, are a good girl."

"Yes," Golda had answered, "but he loves another girl, so what shall I do?"

"Don't worry," said Moishe's mother, and nodded wisely. "There is a great deal more to marriage than mere love."

Could she mean, Golda wondered, the generous dowry her father had given her? Could she mean that?

When Moishe came with his parents that first time, everyone sat around the big polished table and talked. Everyone spoke except Moishe and Golda, who simply looked at one another. Later, when they were married, Moishe described how he had felt. Golda remembered every word; and lying in her bunk, next to the warm little bundle of their daughter's body, she repeated them to herself.

"I felt, Golda, as if all my life was a slate people had written on and that you washed it clean. I looked into your eyes, and I was yours forever. Entirely lost. No one else in the world mattered any more."

It was very, very romantic, thought Golda. And true. How he loves me! And I love him, too. I know I was a little disappointed when I first saw him . . . I had expected someone handsome . . . but he is good, that is what matters in the end. A good man. He will be a good father. She thought of Rachel and remembered how she had looked, dancing with Yasha. For an instant, she imagined what it would be like, to be in his arms, for a tiny moment a small voice in her head whispered: it isn't fair, why should such things happen to her, skinny and pale as she is?

Golda hurriedly pushed such thoughts to the back of her mind and laughed and whispered to Sarah: "Your mother is greedy, that's what she is. Greedy and wicked. But not really. No, I wish them both good luck, truly and honestly. Soon, we'll be with Papa, and then I shan't be greedy any more."

Rachel woke up toward dawn and lay staring into the gray light for a long time. Perhaps, she thought, it was the brandy. Also, there is no one else, and he must be bored and want a little excitement. It doesn't have to mean anything. Maybe he was carried away. I must not think it means anything. Today, he will realize what he has done and maybe apologize. Or I should apologize. I let him. I wanted him to. Was it the wine with me, and the starlight and the black water all around? Or could I love him? She closed her eyes and remembered his lips on the back of her neck. My body was like a cold room on a dark morning, she thought, and then he kissed me and I felt as though a fire had been lighted inside me, and I could feel its warmth and glow spreading through me.

Tomorrow, today, I will keep away from him in case he has changed his mind.

Yasha

There's the dawn. Pale gray light behind us, and the dark is draining out of the sky. I wish Rachel were still here. I wish she could see this sky like pearls, these thin, high clouds, and all the sea around like silver. She will probably never speak to me again. I should never have kissed her. She will run away from me like a startled animal. A few days ago, I would have said: who cares? She is not what I pictured I would want. But last night, she looked like a flower, and her face, when she danced, like a flower opening, and when I kissed her hair (all night I've been trying to remember) did she press herself closer to me, or did I imagine it? Can I smell the smell of her skin still, on this jacket? Where have all my dreams gone, of smartly dressed ladies with diamonds on their fingers and feathers in their hair? My head is full of pictures of Rachel: holding Golda's baby, running along the deck, laughing with Mina, and dancing. Dancing, round and round, next to me, part of my flesh. And her hair in my hands and my mouth on her neck. The wind is blowing on my face, filling my lungs, and still I can hardly breathe for thinking about her.

Chapter 8

"MINA, FOR PITY'S SAKE, LEAVE ME ALONE WITH YOUR crazy talk of horses at a time like this!" Hannah's eyes were filled with tears. "Can't you see that your brother is sick? Can't you see Mrs. Zussmann trying to ease his fever with a cold compress? Can't you understand?"

Mina stamped her foot in rage. "It's you who doesn't see, Mama. You who can't understand. It's because he's lost his horse that he's sick at all. If we can find it, he'll get better. I know he will."

"So what do you want me to do? Leave my poor son and go looking for horses?" Hannah turned back to the bunk.

"I'm going to look. Daniel will help me. You understand nothing. Nothing at all." Mina left her mother and Clara and went to find Daniel.

Mina spoke to Mrs. Katz as politely as she could. She had left her till last because she disliked her so much. All the morning, Daniel had helped her look for Eli's horse. Everyone had been very kind, unpacking their bundles, searching in their bedding, offering help, but the horse had not been found.

"I'm sorry to bother you, Mrs. Katz," Mina said, "but we've lost a horse. My brother's horse. We've been looking for it all morning."

"Ah, so that's it." Mrs. Katz smiled. "I wondered why you were pestering everyone. I thought: perhaps she is practicing to be a customs inspector."

"Could you look in your things for it, do you think?"

"There's no horse in my luggage, girl. I promise you that." Mrs. Katz sniffed.

"Yankel, then . . ." Mina looked around for the boy.

"He's up on the deck."

"May I look in his bunk? In his bundle? Please. It's very important. Eli . . . he's so sick."

"Certainly not. I'm not having nosy strangers poking about among our things. Go back to your own side of the compartment and stay there."

If Mrs. Katz had spoken more kindly, if she had shown the smallest feeling of sympathy for Eli, if she had offered to look herself, perhaps Mina would not have done what she did. She strode forward, seething with an anger that made her hands, her voice, her whole body shake, and tore the blankets from Mrs. Katz's bunk.

Turning to the woman, she shouted at her, "I promised my brother I'd search every corner of this hovel for his horse, and I will, and I'd just like to see anyone try to stop me!"

Mrs. Katz was jumping up and down and yelling, "Get away from here, you terrible girl. Stop! Leave all that stuff alone. How dare you? It's my bed. Stop. Stop! Someone stop her!"

A crowd of people had gathered around Mrs. Katz. Mina climbed up onto Yankel's bunk and started pulling it apart. From somewhere far away, she could hear voices, disconnected, jumbled voices: "What is she doing? . . . She's gone mad . . . lost her temper . . . where's the mother? . . . sick . . . brother . . . horse . . . yes, but still, someone should do something . . . call the captain . . . send for the steward . . ." The noise rose and fell as Mina lifted Yankel's pillow. There was Eli's horse. The wheels and tail had been torn away from the body, and the head had been snapped off. Even the tiny pointed ears had been neatly removed and laid with all the rest of the bits. Mina sat and stared at them in silence. Not a muscle, not an eyelash moved, but her mind was racing.

Yankel had stolen the horse. He had put it under his pillow. They would say it was a joke, that he meant to give it back, but the ways in which it had been destroyed . . . nothing like that could have happened by accident. Yankel had done it. Mina came out of her dream. The people crowded around Mrs. Katz had fallent silent.

"Your son," said Mina quietly, "is not only a thief, but a destroyer. He has stolen and broken my brother's horse."

"Yankel? A thief? Never!" said Mrs. Katz. "How do I know your brother didn't do that himself? He's capable of it, such a child." She whispered to a woman standing beside her, loud enough, deliberately loud enough for Mina to hear: "Not quite right in the head, you know."

"I'll go and find your precious son," shrieked Mina, "and he'll tell me. And then he'll tell you. And then you'll laugh on the other side of your face."

Someone shouted out: "What's all the fuss about? It's only a toy after all."

Mina ran to the door, clutching the broken pieces of Eli's horse in her hands. Daniel followed her.

"Mina, wait . . ."

"Don't you start on me, Daniel. You're supposed to be my friend."

"I am, only wait. Let me come with you to find him."

"I'm finding him. And when I do, he'll be sorry. Here. Take these bits and put them somewhere. Somewhere safe. And then come." She ran up the companionway.

Daniel went to his bunk and put the splintered wood into his bundle. How would they tell Eli? What would he do? Perhaps it was lucky that he was too sick now to care about anything. I must find Mina, he thought. If she finds Yankel and I'm not there, she'll tear him limb from limb. He'll fight with her, too, and he's not weak by any means. I must find her.

"Rachel, can I speak to you?" Yasha stood beside Hannah Isaac's bunk, in which Eli had been placed.

"Yes, but quietly. He's asleep now, but he wakes from the fever, and then he needs someone here next to him."

"Where is his mother?"

"There. With Clara looking after her. She is resting now, so I'm helping." She turned over in her hands the damp rag with which she had been wiping Eli's forehead. "Mina has gone to find Yankel. I don't like to think of what will happen when she does. She is so hot-tempered."

"I heard about the horse," Yasha whispered. "I'm sorry."

"Yes," said Rachel. There was nothing else to say. She had seen the pieces from far away as Mina gave them to Daniel. What kind of child was it who would do a thing like that? Why? What would he grow into? Rachel trembled at the thought.

"Is there anything I can do?" Yasha asked. "For you? For Eli?"

"It's kind of you, but no, I don't think—"

"Rachel?"

"Yes."

"Will you walk with me later? On the deck. When you can."

Rachel bent her head. "I don't know. I can't think properly now. I didn't sleep so well."

"I didn't sleep at all. I stayed by that railing all night."

He was regretting having kissed me, Rachel thought. He wants to apologize.

"Tomorrow, Yasha," she said. "Tomorrow I'll talk to you."

He looked so dismayed that she smiled. "Don't worry. There's no need to apologize for anything. I didn't mind. I won't expect anything. I know it was—" she hesitated—"just the occasion. Perhaps we both had too much of Mr. Kaminsky's brandy."

"Rachel, you don't understand. I don't want to apologize. I'm not sorry. I only—"

"What, then?"

"I only want to make sure—" Yasha fell silent.

"Make sure of what?"

"Sure that you weren't angry with me. Sure that you knew, really knew, I was . . ." He searched for the right word. ". . . sincere."

"You don't regret it, then?" Rachel was speaking so softly that Yasha could only just catch the words.

"Regret it? Oh, Rachel, if you knew." He crouched down beside her, so that his head was near her knees, and looked up at her. "When I kissed you . . . I've been thinking of it all night, looking at that one moment all night, like a treasured picture . . . Rachel, please come and talk with me. Come now."

"I can't come now." She shook her head. "I have to stay with Eli. Maybe later." She turned and stroked Eli's hot, dry brow with the rag, even though the child was sleeping, because Yasha's hair was too near to her hands and her fingers longed to touch it. At last he stood up.

"I'll wait for you." He smiled. "It doesn't matter how long you are."

"You should sleep," Rachel said, "if you haven't slept the whole night."

"Sleeping is a waste of time," said Yasha. "Who needs it?"

"Go now, please," said Rachel. "Hannah Isaacs is coming to talk to me."

"Till later, then," he said. "I'll wait for you."

"Listen, Mr. Kaminsky," said Abraham Klein. "I don't know what to do for the best. Please advise me."

Mr. Kaminsky chuckled softly. "Why do you come to me? Because I am old. Everyone thinks the old are naturally wise, my friend. It is a great advantage we have over the young. Mina Isaacs could probably advise you better, but in any case, speak, my friend. What is the problem?"

"It's Rachel. Did you see them a moment ago? He was talking to her. She looked . . . how can I describe it? Bewitched, entranced. Should I tell her about the marriage I have almost arranged for her? If she knew, she would behave differently towards this Yasha Dubowsky, I'm sure."

Mr. Kaminsky sighed. "Don't tell her," he said. "There are few good things left in the world, and one of them is love. I don't know Mr. Dubowsky, but he seems an honest man. Still, he may have no thought of marriage, and when the ship reaches America, it is quite possible that he will disappear and Rachel will never see him again. Don't make troubles before you have to. It may be nothing, just a romantic friendship. On the other hand, if it is love, then you will have to think carefully about this marriage you speak of and consider how much it means to you and weigh that against your daughter's happiness."

"Thank you, Mr. Kaminsky." Abraham nodded. "That is good advice. Possibly you are 'right and nothing will come of it. After all, we will soon be there."

Mr. Kaminsky said nothing. Speaking had become more and more of an effort and so had sitting up. Clara, thank God, had her hands full looking after the Isaacs boy, or she would have noticed. Mr. Kaminsky put down the book he had been reading. The black letters jumped up and down before his eyes, and his head felt woolly and filled with scraps of memories and dreams. I wonder if this is what dying is like, he thought. If so, it's really not so unpleasant. It could be much worse.

Golda looked down at the filthy creature who was going to feed Sarah.

"Hello," she said. "I'm Golda Schwartz. I'm the baby's mother. Here she is. Isn't she looking lovely now? And it's all thanks to you. I really do thank you with all my heart. You saved her life. I'm sorry I haven't been able to come before but . . ." (Golda silently asked God for forgiveness for the lie she was about to tell)

". . . I haven't been too well. It's the journey. It takes it out of you. I'm sure you understand what I mean."

Why doesn't she answer? Golda thought. She lies there with my Sarah hanging onto her breast, and it might as well be a fly crawling over her. And as for her child, it's a puny little thing . . . and how dirty. Why doesn't she speak? I feel a fool talking to myself like this, but what can I do? I can't sit in total silence. It wouldn't be polite.

"It's very difficult, isn't it," she continued, "trying to keep a baby clean with no running water? I brought so many diapers for Sarah, all made from old sheets and pillow cases torn up. They take up almost the whole of one suitcase, but if you can't wash them properly . . . it's hard, isn't it? Are you going to meet your husband? What a lovely surprise he'll have when he sees not only you, but the baby. A lovely surprise."

The girl said nothing, and Golda retired defeated from the struggle of finding things to say. She sat and waited till Sarah had finished sucking, and then quickly picked her up and held her close. Wrapping a blanket round her little head, now heavy with sleep, Golda stood up.

"Thank you," she said, "I wish I knew your name. I'll bring Sarah again, if I can . . ." She hesitated. Please God, Eli would be better soon, and Clara or Mina or Rachel would bring little Sarah the next time. The smell, the look in the young woman's eyes, the filthy, skinny little baby were more than she could bear.

". . . or maybe one of the others will bring her if I feel weak. Goodbye."

I'm never going there again if I can help it, she thought as she made her way back across the deck. It's not my fault. I don't like things to be dirty and smelly and unpleasant. I like things to be nice. It's my character. And I don't like to think of that woman feeding my Sarah, having milk when I have none. It isn't fair. I don't feel like a proper mother, that's all. And I should. I should be the one. Not her. Not that silent creature with blank eyes.

Olga looked at the wall. How did this woman manage to look as though she had just stepped out of a warm bath? She probably thinks (Olga smiled to herself) that I am always like this. What does she know? There was a time when I was as sparkling as she is. Not so pretty, perhaps. But now this dirt and neglect is like a blanket, protecting me. Eyes slide over you and on to something else when you look as I do now.

"Yankel?" Mina's voice was silky.

"Yes."

"What are you doing?"

"What should you care?"

Horrible, sulky creature, Mina thought. Oh, I'd love to stuff your fat mouth full of cotton wool and glue it up forever.

"I thought you might be gloating over your treasure," she said.

"What treasure?"

"What treasure do you think, stupid? My brother's horse."

"I don't know about a horse. Never seen a horse. What are you gabbling about?"

"Oh, nothing, nothing. Just a few bits of broken horse I found under your pillow a little while ago and showed to about twenty people. Including your mother."

"I don't know anything about it," said Yankel, but fear was in his eyes, and his cheeks had turned the color of white cheese.

"Really? And you expect me to believe that, do you? Spirits took it out of our luggage, did they, and wafted it across to your bed where it very magically arranged itself in a dozen pieces under your pillow. Ha!"

"It was an accident. I never meant to break—" Yankel began, but Mina interrupted:

"So you took it," she whispered. "You're a thief and a liar and fat and ugly, and I'm going to teach you a lesson."

"It was an accident, I tell you." Yankel was whimpering and cowering away as Mina advanced on him.

"I don't care. I don't believe you, and I don't care. I'm going to give you such a kick . . ."

Yankel began to run, but Mina was too fast for him. She caught him around the waist and clung onto the pockets of his jacket and kicked him as hard as she could. He wrenched himself free and grabbed one of her plaits. She slapped him hard across the face, and he kicked her. Wildly, she grabbed hold of his ears and pulled. Yankel howled.

"Stop!" shouted Daniel. "Stop, Mina. You'll kill him."

"I hope I do," Mina muttered and butted her head against Yankel's stomach. He was holding her by both wrists.

"Yankel, let go of her this minute," Daniel said. "Now." Yankel obeyed.

"She attacked me," he said, sniveling. "I didn't do anything, and she just attacked me."

Mina raised her hands again. "Just let me get at him, Daniel."

"No, Mina, stop. It isn't helping. You're just fighting. It won't bring the horse back, will it?"

"No, but it'll make me feel a bit better."

"No, it won't," said Daniel. "Enough. Yankel, did you steal that horse?"

"Yes."

"Why?"

"I don't know. For something to do."

"And did you break it?"

"Yes."

"Why?"

"I don't know." (Because I hate Mina, Yankel thought, because no one ever talks to me, because I'm fat, because I don't want to go to America and see my father . . . because . . . because, who cares why, anyway?)

"Well, you're going to apologize," said Daniel. "To Mina. To Eli. To everyone. You'll tell your mother that Mina was right, and you are a thief. Understood?"

"And if I don't?" Yankel stuck out his bottom lip defiantly.

"We shall go to the captain and tell him you're a thief. There were about a dozen people looking when Mina found those bits under your pillow. I don't think the authorities in America will be delighted to let a criminal into their country. Do you think so?"

Yankel did not answer. He slunk away along the deck. Mina leaned back against the railings.

Daniel said: "Mina? Are you all right. Your face is scratched, and your hair. . . . Do you feel well?"

"Yes . . . a little sore where he hit me . . . but oh, Daniel, he needed to be hit, really he did."

"You would have beaten him to a pulp if I hadn't stopped you."

"I suppose so. I don't know. He was also hitting me and pulling my hair."

"I know . . . look, there's a scratch. Let me clean it a little, or your mother will be worried."

Daniel took a rather dirty handkerchief from his pocket and dabbed at the cut above Mina's eye.

"There, that's better," he said.

Mina, quite suddenly, sat down on the deck and burst into tears.

"Mina, what is it? Please stop. What's the matter? It's not like you to cry."

"I never, never cry," Mina wailed. "Not ever. I haven't cried since I was eight." She put her head between her knees and sobbed.

"Then why? Tell me. Please tell me. Aren't we friends?"

"Oh, Daniel, I'm so worried for Eli. I'm worried all the time, every second. I worry that he's going to die . . . then I worry that they won't let him into America, that they'll send him home all by himself, and who would look after him? I don't know what to do."

"Mina, listen. It's going to be all right. He has a fever, that's all. He'll get better, you'll see." Silently, Daniel prayed to a God he had never completely believed in that Eli should get well. "And of course he'll be allowed in, why not?"

"Yankel said they don't let in . . . mental defectives."

"And Yankel, I suppose, is as wise as King Solomon. What does he know?"

"Isn't it true?" Mina looked up and sniffed.

"Of course it's true. What isn't true is that there's anything wrong with Eli. He's just a little quiet, that's all. A little young for his age, perhaps . . . but if they ask questions, then you can say he's weak from the journey, and besides, he had a fever . . . didn't he?"

"Oh, Daniel, you're marvelous. So clever. Thank you. Of course, if anyone asks, that's what I'll say: 'Oh, he's not himself, sir, no, not at all. He's been ill.' " Mina giggled. "Why didn't I think of that? Come on, let's go and see where Yankel has got to."

Rachel and Yasha were standing in the stern. On the horizon, black clouds were massing like soft mountains, and the sea swelled and rolled in huge gray slabs around the ship, like broken stones.

"There'll be a storm soon," said Yasha. "Rachel, why aren't you speaking? What are you thinking about?"

Rachel looked at him. "I was thinking about Chaim. I would like to tell you about him. Will you listen?"

Yasha nodded.

"I've never told anyone before. Not properly. Not everything."

"I'll listen. Rachel, shall we find a more sheltered place. Aren't you cold?"

"No, no. Please let's stay here." She paused and looked down at the sea. "Chaim was the man I was going to marry. I loved him, and he loved me. It was all arranged. He was to have been with me, on this ship. We were going to start a new life in America. Then one evening, we went walking. It was very quiet. We used to like to walk in quiet streets where there was nobody to see . . . if he kissed me." Rachel blushed. She was speaking so softly that Yasha had to bend his head to catch the words.

"On this day, as we walked, we saw four youths coming toward us. I don't know who they were. They were laughing and stumbling a little. Perhaps they were drunk. As we came up to them, they made a line across the path to stop us. Chaim was holding my hand. They started saying things: horrible things. About me, about what . . . they would do to me, and they kept plucking at my clothes and one of them took my scarf off. I tried to pull Chaim by the hand, tried to make him turn and run the other way. They wouldn't have caught us. They were drunk. He wouldn't come. He hit one of them. On the mouth. I never knew before what a dreadful sound that was, a fist striking a face. It rang in my ears. They all stopped fingering my clothes then and looked at Chaim. They began to close in around him, and he was hitting out at all of them and shouting to me: 'Run, Rachel, as fast as you can, and get help!' I wanted to stay with him. I wanted to strike them, too, for Chaim, and for all the terrible things they had said to me. I felt as though my clothes were slimy where they had touched them, covered with slime like slugs leave when they crawl. But Chaim kept telling me to run." Rachel paused and stared at the horizon. Yasha said nothing.

"So I ran," she continued. "I told my father and a neighbor what had happened, and they took sticks and knives and went to look. I ran after them, but they got there long before me. My father stopped me from coming too near. He stopped me from looking. 'They killed him,' he said to me. 'They murdered him. It's not a sight for your eyes.'" Rachel was weeping now. The tears rolled down her cheeks, and she did not wipe them away. Her voice shook a little.

"They didn't let me see him. I never saw him again. But I've imagined what he must have looked like. I've had dreams. Oh Yasha, I can't bear the dreams."

"Rachel." Yasha took her hands. "My poor Rachel, I don't know what to say. How can I say anything? Only that I wish—" He paused. I wish, he thought, with all my heart that you will let me look after you and love you so that nothing terrible will happen to you ever again.

"I'm frightened, Yasha," said Rachel. "That's why I told you. I'm frightened of loving anybody because

. . . it sounds strange, I can't really explain it . . . everyone I love very much, Chaim and my mother . . . I'm frightened because bad things happen to them. Chaim is dead and my mother is very sick. I don't want more bad things to happen."

"Nothing bad happens because of you," said Yasha. "It's quite enough that they have happened to you, without your feeling guilt as well. Rachel, look at me. Nothing was your fault. Nothing."

"But if I hadn't loved Chaim, he wouldn't have been walking down that street at that time—it torments me, that thought. He would have been in Kracow, far away."

"If, if, if!" Yasha laughed. "If you had wings and feathers, you'd be a bird. You can never say that, never. Don't you see?"

"Yes, I suppose so."

"Rachel, listen. We are nearly there. In America. Speak about that. Speak about the future. The past is gone. It can't come back."

He began to tell her about the jeweler's shop that he would own one day. He described the gems so clearly that she could see them spread out before her. He made her smile as he spoke of the fine ladies and gentlemen who would come into the shop and mimicked the way they spoke and behaved. Behind them the sky was dark, and the wind was rising.

"I must go back to Eli," Rachel said at last.

"Are you feeling better?"

"Yes, Yasha. You always make me smile. It's easy

to smile when you're talking."

"Rachel . . ." He leaned towards her, but she had turned away.

"Yes?"

"Till later."

"Yes . . . later."

He watched her walk along the deck, and a great anger seized him. Why had he said nothing properly, done nothing? He should have held her in his arms and kissed away her tears, and instead, what had he done? Clowned and talked and made her smile. Why am I so clumsy when she's here, he thought. Why can I not say what is really in my heart? Next time, he promised himself, next time will be different.

Golda

*It's so cold out here, but I have to get the smell of the
compartment out of my nostrils for a moment. How
do Rachel and Mina stand it? The wind tears at your
hair and messes your clothes and fills your nose with salt
and water. How can anyone love the sea? It's just a
great, gray lump of water moving about. Nothing to
look at: no trees, no houses, no people, nothing.
Emptiness. The sky is almost black. Perhaps it will rain.
Maybe it will snow. How happy I will be when the
floor stops moving around under my feet. It's not
surprising so many people are sick. It can't be good
for them, all this rolling about. I wish I were in a
warm room, with curtains and a fire, and Sarah in a
cradle. Rachel has gone to look after Eli again. She
looked strange. She had been crying, I think. I must
find out. Please God, don't send us a storm. Not
on top of everything else.*

Chapter 9

MOANS AND SHRIEKS FILLED THE AIR. BUNDLES SLID across the filthy floor. Food left in bowls slopped over onto the planks, onto bedding. The wind howled around the ship, waves flung her weight from side to side, and she creaked in all her timbers as though at any moment she might crack open like a ripe nut. Children were crying, and their parents were crying too as they tried to soothe them.

Hannah closed her eyes for a moment. Everyone is being so kind, she thought: Rachel, Clara, even Golda when her baby is asleep, taking turns to look after Eli so that I can rest. They don't realize that I cannot sleep. I cannot sleep for worrying. We are able to do nothing for Eli, just keep him from burning up with the fever by stroking his face with a rag dipped in water. We feed him with spoonfuls of boiled water begged from the steward. And now this storm has come. If it had happened while Eli was still well, I would have been cowering, terrified and seasick, in my bunk; but now I don't care. The noises all seem very far away, and as for the motion, I hardly notice it. I listen only to the sounds of Eli's breathing, and the movements that he makes are what I see. From time to time he wakes up and whispers a few words, but they make little sense. The fever has made him delirious. Once he sat up in the bunk and clutched my arms and said, 'Have you seen them? Have they gone?' That was all, and then he lay down again. But he has always seen things, even as a tiny child. Imagined them. If there is water, he thinks about what lies below the surface. Once, I found him digging with a spoon around the peach tree that grew against the wall. My favorite tree, whose branches spread out against the gray stone like the sticks of a fan and like a lace fan in the springtime.

"What are you doing, Eli?" I shouted. "Leave that tree alone. Why are you digging there?"

"I'm looking for the very beginning of the tree. Perhaps there is a peach down there, and this tree grows from it."

I tried to explain about seeds and stones, but his eyes clouded over. After that, I grew carrot-tops in saucers and left beans in water to sprout and even planted a lemon pip, but that never grew. Hannah opened her eyes. If Eli lives, she vowed, I will never complain about anything, ever again.

In his bunk, Mr. Kaminsky was only dimly aware of the havoc all around him. Clara sat beside him, holding his hand, trying to keep her balance as the motion of the ship threatened to send her toppling to the floor.

"There's a storm," she said. "You've never seen such a mess. Everything thrown everywhere. Can you hear the shrieking? They think their last hour is come."

"Clara," Mr. Kaminsky's voice was soft. "Clara, will you ask Mr. Klein to say Kaddish for me?"

"Kaddish? What nonsense! You're a long way from death still."

"You shouldn't try to humor me. I know. I'm not a child."

"I'm sorry. Only you have given up. I know you have. You should try. Try to live."

"No, no, it's better like this. Clara?"

"Yes."

"Please see that the captain buries me at sea."

"At sea? But your family, won't they . . ."

"Would you like, Clara, to receive such a parcel? One dead old uncle whom you have never seen? A gift like that, all the way from Europe? And think of the forms to fill in, the questions, and the waiting in huge

sheds for hours while officials look into all the details
. . . I wouldn't do such a thing to them. I don't know
them, but I wouldn't do such a thing to my worst
enemy."

Tears ran down Clara's cheeks, but she brushed
them away and tried to keep her voice level.

"Don't you want to wait? Don't you want to see
America?"

"And crawl off the ship and drop dead at my
nephew's feet? No, better to go here. Quietly, among
friends."

"Are you in pain?"

"No, no, it's quite comfortable. How is the boy?"

"Still delirious, and weak from no food. Oh God, if
only there were proper food, then he would be better,
and you would be better . . . if only I could feed you
. . . if I could have fed you from the beginning . . . you
could have come to live with us in New York. Among
friends . . ." She looked at Mr. Kaminsky. His eyes were
closed. She bent her head down to hear if his heart was
still beating, but the storm and the weeping all around
her filled her ears. A sudden lurch threw Mr. Kaminsky
against the partition, and he lay where he had been
flung. It was over, Clara knew. Trembling, she covered
him with a thin blanket. Her heart filled with tears for
the old man, but she bit her lip and sat up very straight.
I must go and find Mr. Klein to say Kaddish, and I must
send a message to the captain when the storm is over.
Later, I must go through his bundles. They must be

packed ready to give to the relatives. And then I must take Sarah for her feed. She looked at Mr. Kaminsky lying under the blanket, and unfastening the top buttons of her dress, she tore at the thin fabric with her nails until she had made a long rent in it, the symbol of mourning.

There is a white face there, Eli thought, like a moon. Not Mina. Someone with blue eyes. I can't remember. I am moving so much I think I must be flying. My shirt is on fire. Where it touches my skin I feel burning. I feel burning all over. I wish I could see the water. I wish I could dive into the sea and go down and down and be cool forever.

He opened his mouth to speak, and no words came. Someone, the person with blue eyes, laid something damp on his brow. She spoke to him. Her voice sounded as though it came from very far away.

"Eli? It's Rachel. Are you feeling better?"

(Rachel, that was who it was.) Eli nodded weakly.

"Do you want your mother? Or Mina?"

"Yes."

"I'll fetch them. I won't be long."

Eli lay and waited. Soon Mina would come. There were noises all around; the air was filled with weeping and groaning. There was something that he wanted, something he wanted very much, but when he tried to think what it was, his head hurt and his eyes hurt. I'm dreaming, he thought. I'm dreaming that I'm lying in a cradle and Mother is rocking me and rocking me. Eli fell asleep.

"Daniel, I can't bear it. Come on." Mina wrapped a warm shawl around her head and stood up.

"Where are you going?"

"Up on deck."

"Are you mad? In this? You'll freeze. You'll drown. Waves will carry you away . . . please, Mina, have some sense."

"I've got more sense than anyone else. Come on, what are you afraid of? We won't go near the railings. Can you imagine what it *looks* like, out there?" Her eyes sparkled. "It must be splendid. Fancy being on the Atlantic in a storm, a real storm, and sitting huddled in this box with crying children and wailing old women. You'll want to tell everyone: I saw waves as high as houses . . ."

"They won't be that high, will they?"

"I know a good way to find out. Come on."

"Are we allowed to?" asked Daniel. "I don't know if—"

"Everyone's too busy to notice. Hurry. Button your coat. Wind that scarf around your head."

Daniel followed Mina up to the deck. The force of the wind was so great that they flattened themselves behind a jutting-out sheet of metal and stared at the storm. Mina shouted something, but her words were snatched away by the wind and lost. She made a sign with her hands as if to say "never mind" and turned her attention to the sea.

It was true. Everything they said was true. From where she stood, Mina watched the ship climb and climb a straight black cliff face of water that reared up in front of her eyes. Up and up she went; the poor *Danzig* hung on top of the cliff for a dizzying moment, then plunged down the other side into a sea that had become a range of mountains, melting and heaving into crags and boulders, curling into foam, throwing walls of water across the whole width of the vessel. And the noise of the wind was like all the demons in hell, howling together. It's marvelous, Mina thought. If only I could paint those waves, the way the water looks solid, like stone, the way the clouds lie on the horizon. She clung to the edge of a porthole, pressing herself against the metal wall as yet another mountainous wave covered the sky, covered everything. Daniel was making signals, pointing downwards. In the twilight, he looked pale green, and Mina took pity on him. She had seen what she wanted to see, and if she stood here much longer, perhaps the wind would pluck her fingers loose and sweep her up and away and into the ocean. She nodded at Daniel, and together they made their way down to the compartment.

"Wasn't it beautiful? Aren't you glad we went?" Mina's cheeks were pink from the wind.

"No, it wasn't beautiful. It was terrifying. Still, now you're happy. I'll tell my grandchildren: 'A foolish girl called Mina dragged me up on deck in the middle of a storm and then asked me did I think it was beautiful. She was crazy.' That's what I'll tell them." Daniel smiled.

"You just don't love the sea."

"And you do?"

"Yes."

"Why?"

"Because it changes all the time. Because no one can ever know it all, or see everything there is to see in it. Because it's surprising. Why don't you like it?"

Daniel thought for a moment. "Nothing grows. I like to see things grow. Trees, plants, flowers."

"But things *do* grow," Mina protested. "It's all there, under the surface with rocks and fishes and sea plants of all kinds, a whole world. Only," she added, "we can't see it."

"Then what good is it? If you can't see it?"

"You can imagine it, can't you?"

Daniel laughed. "Why bother? On the land, the beautiful things are seen by everyone. No one has to guess at them. If you have to guess, they might just as well not be there."

"You're impossible," Mina said, "and this is a stupid conversation. I'm going to see how Eli is."

"God," Mrs. Katz remarked bitterly, "is good to me. See, he has sent this storm from nowhere so that I may be spared for a few hours the disgrace of having it known all over the ship that my son is a thief. But don't think . . ." she snarled at Yankel, who was sitting miserably beside her, ". . . don't for one moment think that you won't have to do it. The minute there's peace and quiet, you'll go and apologize to that little brat and his wicked sister, and then I don't want one more squeak from you until we land. Do you understand?"

"Yes, Mother. I'm sorry, Mother." Yankel sniffed. "Mother?"

"Yes?"

"Why is Mr. Kaminsky lying with his head covered? And why is Mrs. Zussmann sitting there with a torn dress . . . Rachel Klein's dress is torn, too, can you see? And look, Golda Schwartz is cutting hers with a knife . . . doesn't that mean . . ."

"Death!" Mrs Katz's eyes widened. "Oh God, protect us, there is death in the compartment . . . Mr. Kaminsky . . . oh, this is a cursed boat. It is an omen, an omen to all of us. We will not survive the night." She turned to Yankel. "You sit there and don't move a muscle." She hurried off to spread the bad news to those who had not heard it. Like a raven, she went from group to group, flapping her skirts and clicking her teeth, and wherever she went silence fell, until at last there was no sound in the compartment save for the wailing of the wind.

That wicked woman, Clara thought. Look at her spreading woe. Spreading unhappiness. She must be stopped. Someone must stop her. No one else will do it, so I will. She stood up.

"My friends," she said in a clear, steady voice. "Mr. Kaminsky is dead. He was very old and very weak, and he died peacefully a few hours ago. The captain will bury him at sea, and Mr. Klein has undertaken to say Kaddish every morning and every evening. There is nothing unnatural about his death. It was simply his time to die. But I want to say this: there are children here and young people, and if Mr. Kaminsky knew that anyone"—she stared at Mrs. Katz—"had been trying to increase the general unhappiness on account of his death, he would most certainly come back and haunt that person forever." The crowd stirred, and Mrs. Katz shuffled back to her bunk.

Clara sat down on the floor. You will forgive me, my friend, she said to him in her mind; you will forgive me for threatening her with your ghost, but something had to be done.

"Mina? Is it really you?"

"Eli? Are you better? You look better." Mina touched her brother's face. "Less hot."

"I feel better. I can talk a little."

"Not too much. I'll talk. Can you hear the wind? There's a terrible storm. Daniel and I went to see it. Tomorrow, I'll draw you a picture of how it looks."

Eli frowned. "Mina, did you find my horse?"

Mina said nothing. "Did you?"

"I found it," she said at last, "but Eli, it's broken into too many pieces to mend."

"Have you got the pieces?" Eli whispered.

"Yes, but it's impossible really . . . I think you should throw them away."

Eli shook his head.

"Papa will make a new horse," Mina pleaded. "Nicer than this one. Maybe with a wagon."

Eli wanted to say: just because you get a newer and better and shinier thing, it doesn't mean you have to throw the bits and pieces of the old thing away, as if it had never existed, but it was too complicated, too many words to place in the right order, so he simply said, "I want the pieces, Mina. Please."

Mina shrugged her shoulders and laughed. "Then you shall have them, all wrapped up in a handkerchief. You shall have anything you want as a special prize for getting better. Oh Eli, I'm so glad, so glad!" She bent and kissed him on the forehead. "Soon we'll be there. Do you know that? Very soon now."

It was not until much later that Mina realized something. Eli had not even wept for his broken horse. She had expected torrents, floods, tempests of tears. He was growing up, or perhaps he was too weak from the fever.

Very soon, now, Daniel thought, this journey will be over. Most people, he knew, couldn't wait to leave the ship, but for him it would be like leaving a family. Perhaps he would never see any of them again—not Rachel nor Yasha nor Mrs. Zussmann nor Eli . . . nor Mina.

I don't believe in letters, he thought. After a while

she will stop writing because she is interested in the things that are near her, and she will forget all about me. The others, they will come to the end of a long journey, and I will start on another straight away. Maybe I shouldn't. Maybe it would be better to stay a little while in New York, learn the language, get used to the new country, new ways . . . and then, later, I will go to California.

Daniel felt as though a great load that he had been carrying had fallen from his back. He lay in his bunk listening to the storm beating against the sides of the ship and thought of Mina, looking with wide eyes at those terrible waves. She thought they were beautiful. Smiling at her folly, Daniel fell asleep.

Abraham Klein sat up on his bunk saying the prayers for the dead. Clara had gone to rest now, and the others, most of them, were asleep. Poor Mr. Kaminsky, to die like this where none of the proper rituals could be observed. He, Abraham Klein, would do the best he could. He had noted the date in the front of his Bible, so that every year he would remember and offer prayers. In a strange land. Abraham thought of the work that was waiting for him. Would Panya's cousin be so obliging, so helpful, if they did not go through with the proposed marriage? The friend, the father of the boy, was a wealthy man. Was it not right that a father should make life easier for his child? Should he not ensure that Rachel have the ease and comfort of money about her, to help her? Oughtn't he to tell her, even compel her, if he could, to make such an advantageous marriage? Was it not his duty? Perhaps, after all, Mr. Kaminsky had been right and nothing would come of the friendship with Yasha. There were, after all, only a few more days.

Abraham pondered and worried over such matters as he sat and wished that the old man were still alive to advise him.

"Rachel, are you still awake?"

"Yasha!" Rachel sat up in her bunk. "What are you doing here? It's the middle of the night. Everyone's fast asleep."

"I know. That's why I waited. I wanted them to be asleep. I couldn't speak to you before, with everyone around."

"But we can't speak now. We'll wake them up. Go back to your bunk."

"No, Rachel, please. Listen. I can't sleep. Please

come up on deck with me."

"Have you lost your reason? It's the middle of the night. There's a storm out there. It's bitterly cold."

"The storm is over."

Rachel heard the silence, felt the smooth motion of the ship. Yasha was right.

"Please come," he said. "Wrap up in blankets and come. It's very important. I will go first and wait for you."

"Very well. I'll be there soon."

Yasha nodded and left her. She pulled on as many of her clothes as she could and, stepping off the bunk, wrapped one of the blankets around her shoulders. She looked at her father. He was snoring. She could hear the sounds of sleep from every corner. She tiptoed across the floor as quietly as she could and crept up the companionway to the deck.

"I'm here," Yasha whispered.

"Yes, I see you. But isn't it dark?" Rachel shivered. "No moon, no stars. It feels as though there's nothing at all out there, just black space all around."

"The sea is there. Miles of it. Wait until your eyes get used to the darkness. Rachel?"

"Yes."

"I want to say something. It's very important, so please don't stop me. It's about the jeweler's shop. I want to tell you this: all that was a dream. I have no money, no work, nothing but my head and my two hands. I don't know if there's a jeweler or even a watch repairer in New York who will employ me. There is no position waiting for me anywhere. Probably I shall have to work at something else, something unskilled. In one year from now, I may have no more than I have today, and today I have exactly nothing. I spent all my money on the ticket."

"I know that, Yasha. But if you are worried, you shouldn't be. You will work hard, I know, and one day there will be money. I don't know why you woke me up in the middle of the night . . . are you frightened? Of America? Of what will happen? Oh, Yasha, and you always talked so bravely of the future, of a new country, new opportunities . . ."

"I didn't know then that I would meet you."

"Me? What have I to do with all this?" Rachel looked at him in amazement.

"I have nothing to give you. No home, no security, no money . . . I would like . . . that is . . . I would like us to be married. There, I've said it." Yasha smiled. "I did not know whether I would have the courage."

Rachel looked down at the deck.

"Are you going to answer me?" Yasha whispered. "Please say something . . . anything . . . tell me if you think . . ."

"Yes," Rachel said.

"What did you say?"

"I said 'yes.' I mean, yes I will marry you." She laughed. "You look as if someone had knocked you over the head with a wooden club. What did you think I would say?"

"I thought you would say 'no.' 'Thank you, but no.' "

"Why did you think that?"

"I don't know your feelings. I hoped, but I didn't know . . . if . . ."

"And your feelings?" Rachel asked. "What are your feelings?"

"I don't . . . I have never . . ." Yasha blushed and took a step toward her. He placed his hands gently on her shoulders and looked down at her. He closed his eyes and buried his face in her hair. His lips made the shape of words, and she felt them, although they were not spoken, felt them against her skin. He stepped back and looked at her.

"Rachel, I love you. I'm going to shout it out. I've never said those words before. I love you. I love you." He was grinning now, and his voice was getting louder.

"Stop! Ssh! You'll wake the whole ship!"

"I don't care. I want to sing. I want to yell. I—"

Rachel put a hand over his mouth.

"Yasha, please! Don't shout!"

"I will, I will. There is only one way to silence me."

"Then tell me." Rachel smiled. "Tell me, and I will silence you."

"Like this," he said, and he put his mouth on hers and kissed her softly. "Like this and like this."

The blanket fell away from Rachel's shoulders as they stood there and lay unnoticed on the deck for a long time.

Later, Rachel whispered, "We must go back. Some-one will see that we have gone."

"You have said nothing," Yasha said. "Do you love me?"

"Yes," she answered. "Yes, I do. I love you."

"In the morning, then," Yasha said, "I shall speak to your father."

Abraham Klein looked at his daughter and sighed. "Are you sure, Rachel? Does he make you happy?"

"Yes, Father, he makes me happy. And . . ."

"What?"

"He makes me feel safe."

"How safe? He has no job, no prospects, no money. How will you both live? Oh Rachel, I worry about you so!"

"We will work, Father. We will both work. We are young and strong and we love one another. Isn't that enough? Please give us your blessing."

Abraham Klein thought fleetingly: I could still tell her . . . I could refuse permission for them to marry . . . if I told her it was her mother's wish, she would listen . . . she would be heartbroken . . . look at her shining all over . . . how? . . . how can I?

"Of course, my child," he said at last. "Of course. I give you both my blessing."

Abraham

*How calm it is after that storm! How pale the sky is:
washed clean. The day after tomorrow . . . if only
Panya were here to see Rachel and Yasha. He loves her.
They look, the two of them, lit up from inside, like
lanterns. If only Mr. Kaminsky had lived to see them
like this. Later today, they will place his body in the
water, and who will remember him? Only Clara and
me. And Rachel, because I will speak of him and
remind her. At first, when Clara told me he had asked
to be buried at sea, I was shocked, but in the end,
what does it matter? You lie under a weight of earth
or a weight of water, and the worms eat you, or the
fish. Does it matter which? There will be no rejoicing
tonight in honor of Rachel and Yasha, out of respect
for the dead, but everyone will be happy in their hearts.
Golda Schwartz will feel she is personally responsible.
My Rachel. Yasha's Rachel. I hope she will always
have reasons to be happy. That is the best I can wish
her, because complete happiness is always out of the
question. Impossible.*

Chapter 10

THE COMPARTMENT SMELLED STRONGLY OF DISINFECTANT. Early in the afternoon, everyone had been herded up on to the deck while sailors with buckets and thickly bristled brooms attacked the floor and the walls and everything else they could reach, trying in an hour to remove two weeks of slippery grime.

"They do it to impress the authorities in New York," said Mrs. Katz. " 'See,' they say, 'how comfortable, how clean, our accommodations are!' Us they treat like cattle: what do they care? But the men in America, they must be favorably impressed."

Yankel wasn't listening. Tomorrow, it would all be over. He would eat proper food from proper plates. He would never see Mina or that stupid brother of hers ever again. Yesterday he had had to apologize in front of the whole compartment. He had felt the eyes of everyone on him as he spoke. They had all been listening, and although he had said what he had to say as quietly as he could, the words seemed to boom out and fill the air. Now, he knew, no one at all liked him. He sensed their coldness when he walked past their bunks. Even his mother was angry. He dreaded to think what his father would say, what his father would do when he was told. He was going to be told. His mother had made that abundantly clear.

"I don't know what Moishe will say to me, really I don't." Golda sighed. "It was real gold, that bracelet. His mother gave it to me on our wedding day. But Rachel, I had to do something, didn't I? I had to give her something after she'd fed Sarah and kept her alive."

"Yes," said Rachel, "of course you did. Moishe will understand. When you tell him everything."

"I felt so terrible for her. She looked so pale, and that poor little baby, so filthy and with hardly any clothes on in this cold. I gave her the bracelet, and I thanked her. I was crying. I couldn't help it. And she spoke to me, she really did."

"What did she say?"

"She thanked me for the bracelet. She seemed quite overwhelmed by it. She kept staring at it and turning it around and around in her fingers. That's all, and then just as I was leaving, she called after me and I went back and she said, 'I am calling my baby Mina. Tell her. The other one. The one with red hair.' That's all."

"Have you told her?" asked Rachel.

"Yes," said Golda. "Of course." She said nothing for a while, trying to think why on earth she should be envious. What did she care what this strange woman called her child? She would never see her again after tomorrow. Let the child be Mina. What difference did it make?

Mina said, "Golda told me. She told me you are calling your baby Mina. I'm so happy. It's an honor."

The woman lay with her face turned towards the wall.

Mina continued, "I've come to say goodbye to you. Won't you turn around and say goodbye at least? Please."

Slowly, the woman rolled over in the bunk.

"Goodbye," she said. "Goodbye, Mina."

"Won't you tell me your name? Please. How can I remember you properly without a name?"

"Olga. And listen, I will tell you . . . everything."

Mina listened as Olga spoke about her life, about how she came to be here, on this ship, about her dreams and her fears for herself and her baby, about the past and the future, about all her feelings during the time she had been feeding little Sarah. It was as though all the words that she had kept locked in her heart during the voyage had been set free and whirled around Mina's head like birds.

When Olga stopped talking, Mina said, "There! I knew you could speak. Why didn't you start sooner? We could have talked and talked . . ."

Olga shook her head.

"No, no, but I hope . . ."

"What?"

"I hope my Mina will be like you."

Mina laughed. "Don't wish such a thing! A red-head like me? What a terrible thing!"

"I'm not talking about hair," Olga whispered. "I want her to be brave."

"Am I brave?" Mina was astonished.

Olga nodded and fell silent again.

"I have to go now," Mina said. "My brother has been ill. I have to look after him a lot. He's very weak still. I'll say goodbye. Perhaps we will see each other in America."

Olga shook her head. "Goodbye," she said, and turned to face the wall. Mina knelt down beside the bunk and put her arms round the thin shoulders.

"Goodbye, Olga. Try to be happy," she said and kissed the back of Olga's head. Then she stood up and ran out of the compartment. Her eyes had misted over with tears, and in her throat there was a thick feeling, like a lump of sadness that wouldn't go away however hard she swallowed.

Clara had put Mr. Kaminsky's bundle with her own. So small, it was. It made her want to weep in a way she had not wept either at Mr. Kaminsky's death or at his funeral. A few books, a few threadbare clothes, a pair of brass candlesticks, and that was all. No Bible, no prayer book, no fringed prayer shawl. Mr. Kaminsky had clearly not been on speaking terms with God, and Clara was not surprised. But after a life of nearly eighty-five years, full of work and pleasure and sorrows and memories and children—was this really all that was left? This tiny bundle?

He is still very weak, Hannah thought, but Mina and Daniel are taking turns to walk with him around the compartment, every few hours. Will he be able to walk tomorrow? I know how it will be: hours of waiting, of sitting on suitcases, just like before. They are sitting already, some of them, their bags all around them as if the waiting had begun, and we do not arrive until tomorrow. Will they sit like this the whole night long?

Rachel put the carved wooden box that Yasha had given her between some sheets to keep it safe. In America, they would have a photograph made to send back to her mother. It will make her happy, Rachel thought, to know I am so happy. As soon as we are settled, I will write to her. She put Mina's portrait of her carefully into the pages of her father's Bible, so that it should not become creased. Some of them, she thought, are frightened. You can see by the way they are already holding their documents and looking at them, making sure everything is in order. America: they have heard so much about it, so many stories, like the stories they hear about the Heaven we will go to when we die. Crossing over from one life to the next is a little frightening, a little like dying.

"Perhaps," said Abraham Klein, "my wife's cousin will be able to find work for you as well. Now that you are to be one of the family."

"Perhaps." Yasha nodded. He thought, And what is to become of my dream of a jeweler's shop with sparkling glass windows? I must find a good jeweler and work for him. Start at the beginning, bending over the insides of watches like before. But not forever. One day, he vowed, one day I will give Rachel brooches and necklaces and a ring for every finger.

"Mina?"

"Yes."

"I want to ask you something," said Daniel.

"What is it?"

"That picture, the one you drew of California, with me on the horse . . . could I keep it?"

Mina did not answer. That was the only picture she had drawn of Daniel. She would have to draw another, or how would she remember, when he was so far away, what he looked like? Finally, she said. "Yes, but you know . . . I have no other picture of you. May I draw you again?"

"You won't need pictures," Daniel said, "because I'm not going to California."

Mina jumped to her feet. "Not going? Why not? Oh, Daniel, I shouldn't say it, you've wanted it so much, but I'm so glad. Tell me why not."

"I think I should stay a little while in New York," he answered, "till I learn the language at least. Don't you?"

"I do, I do. That's marvelous. I'm so happy, Daniel, really happy. Will you come and see us? Will we see each other?"

"Yes, of course. That's the other reason I'm not going at once."

"What is?"

"That I'd miss you. I'd be lonely, all by myself."

"Would you really? Miss me, I mean."

"Yes." Daniel blushed. "I would miss you a lot."

Mina looked away. "Then you like me? Really like me?" Her heart was bumping up and down in a most peculiar way.

Daniel nodded. "I like you," he said, "better than anyone."

"And I like you," Mina cried, "and I'm so happy!" She flung her arms around Daniel and pulled him to his feet; together they whirled around on the deck, laughing; round and round until they were dizzy and fell back against the railings.

Daniel said, "I'm completely out of breath now. I like you, Mina, it's true, but you're very exhausting. Very, very exhausting indeed."

Mina closed her eyes. Everything is perfect, she thought. He likes me, and he's not going to California, and Eli is better, and I feel as if I could leap into the air and fly, just like a bird.

That night, everyone in the compartment slept fitfully, waking up every few hours to see if morning had broken.

It must be early morning, Mina thought. She sat up and looked around. The others all seemed to be asleep. She slid out of the bunk and jumped down to the floor as quickly as she could, then tiptoed carefully around piles of luggage, marveling at everyone else's calm. Ever since yesterday when Daniel told her that he was going to stay in New York for a while, she had had a pleasurable feeling deep in her stomach, like before a birthday, a feeling that something wonderful, something miraculous was going to happen, that everything from now on would be good. Why had no one else felt like that? She wondered briefly if she should wake Daniel and then decided not to. There was probably nothing to see yet.

The deck was entirely deserted. The dawn was breaking, yellow light just showing along the eastern horizon. The west was still misty, still half dark. Mina stood and peered into it, every moment imagining that a cloud or a wave very far away was the outline of the land. The sun was rising, a real sun, and the sky was clear: blue and transparent. It was cold, but there was almost no wind and the surface of the sea was only gently ruffled. Mina gazed at the western horizon as the light grew stronger. That thin line of gray just above the water, was it a cloud? Or could it be . . .

"It is!" Mina shouted out loud. "It's America! There it is. I've seen it! I'm the first one of all. It's really America at last." She stood there for a long time as the smudged gray marks, still so far away, took on a more definite shape. Then she turned and ran all the way back to the compartment, nearly falling down the steps in her excitement.

She stood in the middle of the floor and looked at the huddled bodies stacked on their bunks all around her. I've seen it, she thought, hugging herself. I've seen it, and they've seen nothing.

She shouted out suddenly, "Wake up! Wake up, everyone! It's there. America. You can see it now. It's really there. How can you sleep? Wake up. You can see America."

Heads were lifted from pillows, arms were stretched, and gradually the drowsy murmur that filled the compartment changed to an excited babble as they took in the news. One after another, they collected their belongings and struggled out on to the deck to see it. To see America.

There it is, thought Yasha. There, at last. When I rode on the wagon, running away to the nearest railway station, watching the mud churn under the wheels, watching the trees dripping in the rain, did I really believe that it would be like this? So many high buildings, so much stone and concrete? There must be people here in the thousands, like insects, like ants. Can any person, can anybody's life really matter when the buildings are so tall?

Daniel thought of California, of all that he had heard and read about the warmth and the fruit trees and the mountains. California would be many different colors. This was gray, entirely gray, but perhaps that was only in the early morning and from a distance. The colors would maybe be clearer later on. That was the Statue of Liberty. How lovely she was with the sunlight on her, how huge and brave and comforting, like a sentinel holding up a torch to keep the darkness away.

Somewhere, in one of those buildings, thought Golda, Moishe is preparing for me to come home. He has cleaned the rooms and bought cakes, maybe even flowers and some wine. He's probably waking up now and putting on clean clothes. He has taken the day off from work. He is singing as he washes and dresses. He will see Sarah for the first time. Oh, Moishe, where are you among all those thousands of people. I want to see you again. I want to walk on dry land.

Today, thought Clara, is the last day of the voyage. We put down our lives, like suitcases, for a few days, and tomorrow we take them up again. All the things that were of such importance to us here on the ship will fade into insignificance before the problems and pleasures of real life. That's where life is, there, on land.

This has been an interval, a space between two worlds, and when it's over, it will be like a dream. For Mr. Kaminsky, one life was enough. Perhaps he was right. Perhaps two lives is one too many. But who has the choice? You go on, that's all, and whatever happens, happens. I don't know if I will even recognize my son any more.

Eli still looks so pale, Hannah thought. How will he find his way in such a huge country? Even the village was difficult for him. And how will he survive a new school, learn a new language, become an American? Mina. Mina will be happy. She will learn the new ways and stride out to meet everything, just as she always does. She will forget the old country in the end, because there will be so much to see. Hannah felt a small tremor of fear run through her and then subside. Soon her husband would be with her again, to protect her. And there would be a piano.

As the *Danzig* steamed towards the dock in the sunlight, under a clear sky, as the idea, the dream of a new world took shape on the horizon, Mrs. Katz was thinking of soap and water.

The first thing, she thought, will be a good bath. We will both need scrubbing from top to bottom to get rid of all the dirt. And everything will need to be washed: all the clothes and the bedding, everything, to get the smell of this dreadful ship out of them.

Look at everybody, thought Yankel, strung out along the railings, crowding to get a better look, gawping and exclaiming about everything. What's there to see? Buildings, that's all. What's so special? The fuss they're all making, you'd think the whole place was full of castles and rainbows, like fairyland. It's just a place, that's all.

I have no idea of what I shall do, or where I shall go, when I step off this ship, Olga thought. There was a certain pleasure in being at the mercy of Fate, like a feather lifted on the wind. Perhaps I could become a maid in a wealthy household. Perhaps somewhere where there is another baby. I will look after the two of them and wear a proper dress. Maybe even a white lace cap. And my Mina will be an American. She will speak English. Suddenly Olga shivered. Dear God, she prayed, don't let her grow up a stranger to me. I am just beginning to love her as she should be loved.

Rachel's eyes were filled with unshed tears. If only Mother could be here, she thought, if only she could see this sight. Everything sparkles, everything is shining. The sun is so bright it might almost be spring. Yasha looks like a child opening a marvelous gift. I wonder how many people are remembering the lovely places they have left behind? When will I see another field with plum trees and apple trees growing beside it and a stream running through it? Only in my dreams.

How did they do it, Mina wondered, looking at the Statue of Liberty. How did the sculptors make the model? What did they use, carving the shape out bit by bit as they went, first the draperies, then the arms and neck, and then the head. How did they cast the metal, when the model was made? It seemed to her a miracle that something like this could happen, that all that metal could become the figure of a woman. I will ask Papa to teach me to carve wood, she resolved. Why have I never thought of it before? That's what Eli's horse was once, a part of a tree. Will Eli remember everything that I have told him? I must not lose him in the crowd. I shall stay right next to him till we find Papa.

By the middle of the morning the deck was so crowded that there was hardly room to move. Mina noticed that Clara was sitting on her suitcase, dressed in her fur hat, wearing gloves over her rings, just as she had at the beginning of the journey. Rachel and Yasha were holding hands and talking. Mina thought: they don't even care about America. All they care about is one another. They could be going anywhere. Golda stood beside Mr. Klein, holding Sarah up so that she, too, could see the square towers, all different sizes, rising up before them, bathed in sunshine. She looked for Mrs. Katz and Yankel but they were nowhere to be seen. Perhaps they had moved further back. Briefly, she caught a glimpse of Olga and little Mina, and then some people moved forward, and they were hidden from view. What a lovely day it was, almost like spring. It was surely a good omen to arrive on such a day.

Hannah kept her eye on Eli, who was scarcely visible under wrappings and blankets, sitting between Mina and Daniel, his eyes wide.

"I never thought America would be like this," he whispered to Mina. "Look at that huge lady holding a torch. Why do they put a statue there?"

"It's the Statue of Liberty," said Daniel. "It's supposed to be like a welcome."

The statue terrified Eli, but he said nothing. Why were there sharp spikes sticking out all round the head? Why were the eyes so blank? He couldn't understand why Mina admired it so much. Secretly he was disappointed because America was not as pretty as he had imagined. Gray. Tall buildings like straight boxes sticking out of the water. He stared at the sea.

"Mina," he said at last, "Mina, look."

"What's the matter, Eli? Aren't you feeling well? What are you looking at?"

"At the sea," Eli said. "Right over there. It's blue, isn't it? Really blue."

"Blue enough," said Mina, looking into the distance where the water was the color of a dark sapphire. "Not exactly what I expected, but blue enough."